To J-9,
with love,
Jan

Birds of a Feather

Short Stories and Personal Essays
Inspired by a Gay Life

By Jackson Lassiter

Cover art courtesy of Anthony Dortch (copyright © 2012 Anthony Dortch).

Short stories and personal essays in this book (some in different versions) have appeared in the following places:

"A Critter in the Henhouse," *Heartland Review* 2006, and as "The Night Beast" in *Edifice WRECKED* 2006.

"Purple Glass," *Gertrude V17.*

"Near Miss," *Best Gay Love Stories 2007.*

"Good Weed, Bad Deed," *Ink and Ashes 2005* and *South Loop Review V8.*

"Slices," *Prime Mincer 2011.*

"The Rapture," *Gay City: Volume I, 2008.*

"Birds of a Feather," *Harrington Gay Men's Literary Quarterly V8.*

"Swimming Upstream, June Cleaver on my Mind," *Silver Boomers V1.*

"A Fistful of Serenity," *Gay City: Volume 2, 2009.*

"While Waiting for my Beloved's Arrival at Sacramento Int'l Airport," *Apocalypse Literary Arts Magazine 2007.*

"Cherry: The Fat Man's Story," as "Cherry", *Big Tex[t] 2004.*

"Walking the Blind Dog," *Yalobusha Review 2010.*

"At the Sex Party," *Gay City: Volume 3, 2010.*

"Dose of Reality," *Tidal Basin Review 2011.*

"Natural Selection," *Jerry Jazz Musician 2005.*

"Ay, ¡Caramaba!, Papi," *Sin Fronteras: Writers Without Borders V13.*

Visit the author's website at *http://www.wix.com/luckyjrl/jackson-lassiter#!*

Contact the author at *luckyJRL@hotmail.com.*

ISBN-13: 978-1475103083
ISBN-10: 1475103085

This collection is dedicated to the memory of
Shirley Ilene Mowell Lassiter,
who taught me to love words at an early age.

CONTENTS

THE SHORT STORIES

THE PERSONAL ESSAYS

PROLOGUE

WHAT I WAS TAUGHT
WHEN I WAS TEN

In the late spring of 1968, my father taught me how to coax perfect vegetables from Wyoming's rocky soil. We grew slender orange carrots with drooping ferny tops and lavender-tinged turnips and beets the Cordovan color of his rarely-worn dress boots. We created potatoes gnarled like living rocks. Together we babied water-hoarding melons and cantaloupes. We tended sweet corn and tomatoes and peppers and eggplant, we herded kohlrabi, cabbage, lettuce, beans and peas toward the dinner table, and yanked radishes like tiny, biting red pearls from the unforgiving clay. My father taught me how to work the earth and make her produce. I learned that something necessary can

1

come from nothing more than dirt and water, hard work and perseverance.

Later that summer, he taught me how to break a wild three-year-old mare into a docile saddle horse. I worked with the filly daily, gently. My father taught me to first rub along the horse's dangerous legs and over her muscled withers with the underside of a thick wool saddle blanket, its Navaho pattern stiffened with the dried salt of a thousand sweaty rides. When the mare grew accustomed to the feel of the thing, he told me to rest its weight on her quivering back. And then the saddle, first just passed over as if it were a rare and welcome breeze in the August heat, then cautiously settled atop the blanket. All the while I murmured to the nervous filly, mimicked my father's spurious monotone.

"That's a good horse, sweet baby, nothing's going to hurt you here. Sweet filly, good baby." Over and over I soothed her as my father instructed, until she trusted that the saddle was harmless.

And then he had me to tighten the cinch with a quick move and use a strap to twice raise the hair across her sleek, dun butt. She startled and bucked like an equine devil. Her brittle hoofs rose and then slammed to the hardscrabble corral surface over and over and over again, the sound an ominous drum beating against my head. And when she began to tire, my father made me throw a rock and yell a profanity – "buck, you sumbitch, buck" – to bring the devil back to life, to exhaust it, to exorcise it.

By the fall of 1968, he had taught me to hide my delicacy. He did this by showing me how to coddle 600 peeping one-day-old chicks whose only mothers were me and a low-slung heat lamp, and when they reached adulthood, how to one at a time hold their wingtips and feet in my left hand and lay their necks across the chopping block, to make my right hand swing the axe with clarity.

I learned how to sit quietly, my back pressed against the rough red bark of a lodge pole pine high in the Big Horn Mountains, to watch a sagebrush-scented trail where rutting mule deer bucks chased the does, to aim for a spot in the distracted fella's ribcage just behind the front leg. I was taught to hold the rifle steady as I pulled the trigger, and how then to eviscerate the carcass with just a few, swift moves.

In November, he told me that I should scratch the arthritic old Collie behind the ears before he took her to the backside of the barn and put a .22 gauge bullet in her head.

In the winter of 1968, unending waves of glacial air slid down from the Canadian Rockies and shoved the permanent snow into massive drifts. We were buried inside, scuttling out only to feed the frost-covered livestock and haul in more firewood. Ensconced near the fireplace, the smoking remains of a fallen Cottonwood heating our country living room, my father taught me every joke he knew. He told jokes about wops and japs and darkies and kikes and gooks and polacks and beaners. His punchlines targeted frogs and retards, fat girls, skinny whores – krauts and Jews and Arabs. And I understood that every one of them was less than any of us. But when he got to jokes about faggots and queers, the acrid Cottonwood smoke brought tears to my eyes and the Canadian wind gave me chills.

My father was not a bad man. He was a good man doing the best he could given his own upbringing and the cultural norms of where we were. Still, inadvertently, when I was ten my father and my

community taught that I was the least of all, and it's taken a lifetime –
my lifetime – to convince myself otherwise. This collection of fictional
short stories and non-fictional personal essays is simply an honoring of
that lifetime. These words are a representation of that journey to self-
acceptance. They are its product.

A CRITTER IN THE HENHOUSE

"Get up, goddammit, something's in the henhouse."

My father's command pierces my sleep like a .22 caliber bullet and I snap fully awake. Our dog, Boots, barks in the distance. I am tangled in sweat-dampened sheets in the dank air of my stifling farmhouse bedroom. It is a hot summer night. August 16, 1975, to be exact. But the movie posters carefully tacked over the wallpaper are from years past. My mother and I used to watch these classics every summer afternoon, and in her absence I find comfort in the familiar, beaming faces of the starlets.

"You're a 14-year-old boy," my father would grumble at the two of us as we watched. "You," he ordered, pointing at me, "turn off that damn old movie and do something a 14-year-old boy does."

But Mom and I just nestled deeper into the sofa.

The digital clock clicks from 3:11 to 3:12 as Boots and my father continue to sound the alarm, a ruckus which includes the frantic squawking of our laying hens.

"Get up, you dumb fuck," he yells. "I'm gonna kick your ass if you make me miss this critter."

I know better than to linger. My father has never been the kind of man to wait patiently, and it's worsened since Mom died last spring. He was just grumpy before, and she could protect me. She kept him human, now he's just down-right mean. And he and I are here alone. He kicks my ass first and asks questions later.

I leap from my bed and grab a 12-guage shotgun from the rifle rack on my way out of the house. I know what's up; this scene has played out before. Hens lay eggs, varmints eat eggs. And hens. They find a way to crawl in the henhouse, no matter what steps we take to deter the night visits. These clever creatures are inventive. They climb over, dig under, or chew through any obstacle we construct. And once inside, neither chicken nor egg is safe.

I don't bother dressing. The thermometer hovers at 90 degrees and no one is going to see me in my Jockeys; the nearest farmhouse sits a good mile over the hill.

I hit the back door at a run but my father is already half-way to the barnyard perched on the rise behind the house. Seems he is always at least one step ahead. He wears nothing but his boxers and unlaced work boots, and he clutches a rifle. The angry sinew of his calves works as he strides uphill toward the outbuildings. He's nothing but bone and tendon; too damn mean for fat to stick.

"Hurry up, boy. Did you get the flashlight?"

6

I turn back to retrieve the forgotten flashlight but he stops me quick.

"I knew I couldn't count on you. I grabbed it; now get your ass up here, pronto."

Like I said, always a step ahead.

We pause at the door to the coop to get organized. Inside the hens flap and fly, screeching and cackling. There's quite a stir in there. He hands me the flashlight and instructs me to hold the beam steady on the beast as soon as I open the door. He whispers but I hear the yell of his intention.

"Just keep the light on it, nothing else, so I can get a shot," he says. The words scrape over his teeth.

"Do you think you can do that, boy?" he continues. Only it isn't a question; it's his assertion of the fact that I probably can't. I've lived with him my whole life and I've learned how to decipher his code.

"Just pay attention," he hisses, but I don't know why he whispers. Boots hasn't stopped barking since this ordeal began and the hens themselves are causing quite a disturbance. The intruder has to be aware that the gig is up.

My father braces for the assault, one leg to the front with bended knee, the other locked straight back for stability. His upper body leans forward and the rifle butt tucks snugly into his shoulder. He lays his right cheek against the wooden stock and sights down the barrel pointed at the still-closed door. He stands ready, and except for the worn white boxers waving slightly in the tepid breeze, he might be a statue: the naked marksman. Or the enemy army's General in one of the old war movies. I am contemplating his role when he commands me back to the task at hand.

"Go!" he yells.

"Go....where?" I ask. My musings interrupted, I am unsure of what he expects.

"Jesus Christ, I mean open the fuckin' door and shine the goddam light."

"Oh," I say.

I stand in the open night wearing nothing but my underwear with a flashlight at the end of one extended arm and a rifle tucked under the other. I imagine this is a funny scene, and if I weren't part of the joke, I might laugh.

"Go now!" he commands.

I tentatively nudge the door open with one bare foot, not knowing what horror will greet me. Wolves? Bandits? Rabid weasels? I swallow my fear, which lodges as a burning sensation right below my navel, and step into the chaos. The smell of chicken shit hits me first, followed by the frightening sound of a hundred panicked hens whirling uncontrollably around the coop. Dull thuds punctuate the repeating crescendos of their squawks as they smash into walls and nesting crates. They fly blindly in the dark, afraid of something they and I can't even see.

I am watching the bright spotlight of the flashlight sweep across the space, searching for the culprit, when suddenly the light careens around the room drunkenly, as though the person holding it has fallen. Too late, I realize that I am the person holding the light, and I *am* falling. Boots, overcome with excitement, has rushed headlong into the coop only to hit me square in the back of my knees, which buckled and tossed me face-first to the muck of the chicken coop floor.

I am definitely not laughing.

From my floor-level vantage point, though, I can clearly see two things. First, the scene is littered with several dead hens, each with the top of her head neatly removed, as if by a skillful surgeon yielding a sharp scalpel. Whatever wreaks this havoc has been in a killing frenzy, overreacting to the easy-picking of penned hens like a food addict might react if given the keys to a pastry shop. Some of the fallen hens still flap and wiggle. Their bodies are not yet aware of the fact that they have been slaughtered.

The other thing I see is a skunk exiting the henhouse via the door I have just fallen through, Boots in hot pursuit.

"Jesus fuckin' Christ, I shoulda' known you would screw it up," my father bellows as he lowers the rifle. "Get up before it gets away."

I extract myself from the goo and follow my father's ghostly figure into the narrow crevice between the chicken coop and the milking barn. Boots barks behind the henhouse and since she barks in place, we deduce that she has cornered the skunk. As we pick our way through the dark passageway, my father cussing in front and me limping along behind, trying to shake off as much chicken shit as I can, I realize that my shotgun aims squarely at his back.

"Fuckin' dog coulda' held the light better," my father mumbles in the shadows ahead. "Might have gotten that fuckin' skunk this time, but no, you had to screw it up. How's that chicken shit bath?" He laughs. First time I've heard him laugh in months.

My index finger slides along the polished surface of the wooden rifle stock to rest on the trigger. It longs to squeeze, and the next morning's scene plays in my mind.

"I fell and the gun went off," I imagine myself explaining to the sheriff as he stands over the remains of my father. The body is nearly torn in half by the close-range shotgun blast. The chicken shit I smeared on it dries in the morning sun.

"What the hell are you giggling about? Get back here, dog's got him holed up under the coop," my father says, interrupting my fantasy as he disappears around the backside of the building. My finger moves away from the trigger.

The henhouse sits on a slight grade, the front resting squarely on the hard packed soil of the barnyard while the backside is elevated about six inches above. Boots says that the skunk has taken refuge in this cave between the floorboards and the soil. She says so loudly and repeatedly. Boots does her doggie dance at the back of the chicken coop.

"Shut up!" my father yells at the dog as he manhandles her away from the opening. He restrains her using the chain collar and orders me to lie on the ground and search under the building with the flashlight. Great, I am thinking. I'm in my underwear, covered in chicken shit, and now I get to lie on the dirt and come face-to-face with an angry and scared skunk. This does not bode well.

"What the hell are you waiting for? Christmas?"

I lean the shotgun against the building and lower myself to the ground. My knee gets scraped in the process but I don't mind: it will be additional proof that I fell when the gun accidentally went off.

"Do you see the sum'bitch?" he asks. "Only good skunk is a dead skunk."

He said these same words last winter when another skunk had visited. Boots and I had both gotten sprayed and we were ostracized to the barn for our tomato juice baths, the country remedy for skunk spraying. My mother tried to tell him that leaving me out in the barn on a cold night, wet, was cruel, but he was having no part of her coddling. They had a big fight about it that ended with her crying. Tomato juice works, alright. Gets the stink out but it sure does sting the eyes.

Particles of dust and bits of feather are suspended in the musty air beneath the flooring, and they sparkle like tiny stars in the bright beam of the flashlight. It's a miniature alternate universe under the chicken coop, a galaxy far away from this depressing farm with its mean-assed farmer. I envy the skunk's ability to enter this world.

As my eyes slowly grow accustomed to the play of bright light and deep shadow in the confined space, the form of the skunk emerges from the darkness. It huddles about six feet in front of me, tucked as far back in the narrow cave as it can get. It peers directly at me.

Better to face the front end of a cornered skunk than the back end.

It blinks as the light crosses its face, and I cannot help but notice its eyelashes: they are a succulent yet delicate frame for the creature's twinkling eyes, and they wave as it winks, conspiratorially. It tests the scent of me, its black button nose twitching as it sniffs. I sniff back. It seems unafraid, as am I. Wonder fills the dusty distance between us as the skunk and I take measure of each other. And then it does something incredible.

Flopping to its side, it exposes its belly as though begging me to notice the swollen, pink nipples that peek from a nest of black hair. She is a mother, and tucked somewhere in a thicket beyond this encounter, she has a family.

"What do you see?" My father's caustic words shatter the wondrous spell and the magic of the moment falls to the ground in a million shards.

"Nothing. It's gone. Must have slipped out some other way."

"God damn you. Next time I say pay attention, pay fuckin' attention."

I stand and we gather ourselves. My father leaves first – one step ahead, as usual – carrying his rifle in one hand and wresting Boots toward the house with the other.

"Come on, bitch," he says. "What the hell's wrong with you? Damn skunk got away. No fault of yours." But Boots knows that the skunk is still there. I can lie to him but the dog knows better. She does as she is told, though. She knows his wrath.

He glares at me. "Wipe that smirk off your face."

He turns toward the house. My rifle once again aims directly at his back and my finger retraces its way to the trigger. I marvel at how easy it would be. One simple muscle contraction. One squeeze of one finger.

I glance back to the barnyard just as the skunk emerges from her hiding spot. She waddles to the cover of reeds along a ditch bank like nothing at all has happened and the last I see of her is the plume of her tail disappearing into the weeds. It waves one last, jaunty "so-long" as she heads home to her babies. I wave back.

I am left to follow my father. The bones of his rail-thin back form an elegant curve as he bends to congratulate Boots on her keen watchdog skills, but when he stands upright again his boxers have bunched up between the flat loaves of his ass. His hands are busy with his rifle and the dog, so he balances on one foot and shakes his other leg to loosen them. As the fabric falls back into place I sigh, and my own rifle points back toward the ground. I'm still a child, but I know enough to understand that life offers choices, and even without such dire action my nights will someday be different. Tonight, though, I can only wait for him to fall back to sleep, and then I'll curl alone on the sofa and lose myself in the late-late feature on the all-night classic movie channel. This is, for now, my only choice.

PURPLE GLASS

August, 1969 – Basin, Wyoming. This town and this time are as far from enlightenment and as close to innocence as anything an eleven-year-old boy will ever know.

It is mid-afternoon. Henry Jackson and I shove through the dense heat on our Schwinn Stingray bicycles, riding a thin ribbon of open highway that links our town to the next, some twenty miles distant. We are headed to the ancient dump ravine, usurped two years ago when the county created a "sanitary landfill" a few miles away. There, the trash is quickly turned under, hidden from sight and lost forever. The old dump and its open-air treasures, however, are left intact.

Townsfolk had tossed their refuse over the rim of the deep, dry gully since time began, left it there to be disposed of by four seasons of harsh weather and generations of marauding country boys. Like Henry and me. Today we will scavenge the heaps for old glass bottles turned purple by the malignant sun. It's a common pastime for boys in these parts – the purple bottles are sold to *Ye Olde Curio Shop*'s owner back in town. The big-city, east-coast tourists passing through here on their way to Yellowstone National Park snap up these relics of "the old west" like cutthroat trout after a flashing spinner lure. We boys appreciate the pocket change.

Henry and I pedal side-by-side along the yellow middle line of the car-less black highway, competing to see who can go the farthest without grabbing the handlebars. We laugh hysterically when one or the other wobbles and threatens to bite the asphalt. We are both shirtless; Henry's back is bronzed and mine is reddened.

A final long grade proves too much for our one-speeds. We dismount and push them toward the crest of the water-starved and mostly barren hill. This is the desert highlands of Wyoming, not the lush alpine of the mountains looming on the horizon. Plant life here is minimal. This landscape of rolling mounds grows little other than uniformly round baseball-sized rocks, deposited by ancient glacial movement, we've learned in our sixth grade geography class. These hills and these rocks have been worn smooth by centuries of slow grinding, and the plants fare no better. Sparse silver sagebrush and dark green rabbit brush squat here and there, drooping in the viscous afternoon heat. Henry plucks a wild onion shoot. It reeks of garlic. He dares me to taste it and when I do, my tongue burns.

We haven't asked permission to rummage for purple glass together. We know better. We aren't supposed to do anything together. Not because we come from different backgrounds, although that would be an excellent first guess. Henry's father is the high school math instructor, at the top of the stack in our little farming community, and Henry usually plays with the popular town kids. My dad works the fields and my friends have always been rough-and-tumble farm boys and other poor kids. But children of our age respond to what feels good; we don't take into account others' notions of normalcy or their judgment of right and wrong. All Henry and I know is that something draws us together. And because of that, we aren't allowed to be friends.

We had played together only one other time. Earlier that year we'd carried his GI Joe action figures to the isolated riverbank, where we made war games in the slanted spring sunlight for the afternoon. We'd crawled through the budding underbrush pretend-bombing until our jeans were caked with soil, not even caring how angry our mothers would be. Finally we laid the man dolls in a bed of new grass, spooning front to back in the delicious sunshine. We followed suit, our cuddling naïve. When dusk threatened, Henry's dad found mine and together they came looking for us. The nestled boys they discovered scared them, and they swore on the spot to nip this ugly blossom. We were never to play together again.

But here we are, consciously ignoring parental censorship – living proof that boys will be boys.

Except for the clinking and scuffling sounds our feet make picking down the garbage-covered hillside, the afternoon hangs silent. We sort through the skeletal remains of trash – everything weather bleached and reduced to its core essence, stripped of life and flesh and odor and color. Except the old bottles, which seem to have wrung the blue right out of the sky, summer day after summer day, until they are as deep-hued as a martin. We search for flashes of purple among rusted tins and mattress springs, broken plates, bodiless doll's heads and grayed wood still in the shape of someone's davenport.

A magpie flaps overhead, her long tail fluttering in her wake. She is disinterested in our treasure hunt, I think, as I watch her cross the turquoise sky. And then I am falling to my butt among the detritus, my scream shattering the rural silence. Henry scurries to my side and as I raise my left foot in explanation, his horrified face mirrors my fear. A fragment of glass – two-thirds of the circular neck of a long-ago-broken and scattered quart canning jar, the ridges for its screw-on lid intact, is clamped around my high-top tennis shoe. One sharp end stabs at the rubber sole. The shard curves perfectly around the outside of my foot, where the other jagged end has sliced through the canvas shoe and tatters the white sock beneath. It disappears into the flesh of my foot.

"This is bad," I moan. "They are going to kill us."

Henry kneels beside me. "Does it hurt?"

"Um, not really."

"What do we do?" Henry asks. The tenderness in his voice gives me courage.

"I gotta get it out."

I take a steeling breath and yank. The glass pulls free. There is no shocking torrent of blood, no hissing like air escaping an impaled, overinflated tire. When I remove the shoe and sock, we are dumbfounded. The glass knife has stopped its slice and dice just short of skin penetration. My shoe has been shanked, my sock has been shredded, but my foot glows pink and healthy – intact – in the brilliant sun.

Henry and I begin to giggle, and then the giggles snowball to laughter, and then we can't stop. Our laughter grows so out of control that we flop spastically on the trash-littered hillside, as helpless as fish lured out of water, gasping open-mouthed in the sunshine until we are finally laughed out and there is nothing left but to catch our breath. We gradually return to ourselves, and as the sun retreats in the west we secret the hilarious memory of our illicit outing home. Alone. We don't mention the incident to anyone, and although our friendship never blooms, we do carry a glistening purple glass intimacy through the rest of our school years.

The last time I see Henry Jackson is at the multi-township dance celebrating everyone's high school graduation. It is now May, 1976. I am leaving the dance, readying to back my Chevy Impala out of the gravel parking lot. Suddenly a fist thrusts through the opened window, just missing my cheek. The hand grabs my neck and squeezes.

"I'm going to beat your ass, fag," one of the graduates from a neighboring town spits.

His face is eerie, cast in long shadows from the blue light of the dashboard. His hair is straggly and his breath stinks of Sloe Gin. I am terrified: I'd never been in a fight, am not even sure I know how to punch. And then I see Henry Jackson striding through the bright spotlight of the car's headlights, like a superhero or a Prince Charming. He marches to my side of the car and grabs the drunk by his shoulders.

"He's not who you think he is," Henry says. His voice is stern. "Come on."

He leads my attacker away and that's the last I ever see or hear of Henry Jackson. I leave our town shortly thereafter and assume a more enlightened and less innocent adult life in a city far, far away. But to this day I sometimes wonder – whatever became of Henry Jackson? Does he remember the day we both believed I'd lost my foot? And who might he spoon with now, on a bed of new grass in the warm spring sunshine?

NEAR MISS

Said Juarez doesn't just walk into Uncle's Lounge, he slithers, like an apparition making an appearance at his own funeral. This is a reasonable entry given the circumstances. As the voice inside his head cautions, "If Mama finds out I'm here, she will kill me."

He creeps through the doorway at the intersection of 18th and Sanchez Streets. All of Uncle's patrons use this doorway, but compared to their ribald, ass-slapping, hey-everybody-look-at-me entrances, the pallor of Said's appearance is eerie. He doesn't so much make an entrance as simply manifest. Not that anyone notices.

It is 9:30 p.m., Saturday, late October, San Francisco, the Castro. These are prime logistics for gay male cruising under any circumstances, and the warmth of an Indian summer tilts the rut to full swing. Eager men cram the small space. Their laughter and repartee – the din of which seems tangible, as if it was a sentient being with purpose and need – parts before Said like Biblical water. It is cleaved by the dagger of unease he brandishes, sliced by the switchblade of his fear (a blade honed by the constant harassment of his ever-present internal dialogue, a voice that sounds remarkably like his mother's).

Said carves out space to stand near the outermost edge of the frivolity. He wafts near the border of the scene, just inside the bar's entrance. He tests the waters. If they chill, he will bolt.

More than fifty men carouse in the long, narrow space of the tavern (every single one of them, Said's inner voice reckons, more handsome than he). Should one of these men cease the carnal pursuit long enough to notice Said, he might observe a pronounced tremble; a shimmering of the heavily-starched, lemon-colored shirttail that drapes over the intentionally baggy jeans. Said adopted this look to camouflage the hefty humps of his ass. That ass niggles; it gnaws at his nerves and it forms the very foundation of his concept of self.

"You're *Mexicano*," Mama Juarez scolded when an adolescent Said fussed about the dimensions of his burgeoning *culo*. The heavy accent tumbled from the downward-drawn corners of her frown as she continued, "We're known for our *traseros grandes*! Besides, *niño*, boys aren't concerned about those kinds of things."

One eyebrow arched in accusation, and she fired a meaning-riddled glance at Said's father, who eavesdropped from the king's perch of his well-worn Barcalounger. But Señor Juarez ignored his son's plight. Eight children preceded Said; seven were high-pitched and raven-haired Latinas who refused to be neglected, the one other son was a baseball-playing-skirt-chasing-replace-the-carburetor kind of boy. A father's quota is sometimes limited, and this father's allotment of caring was already depleted; his youngest son's indelible deviancy permanently locked the deadbolt on his sympathy. Señor Juarez declined to be bothered with this, his last offspring's sense of identity.

"Don't worry, *miho*," was Mama's final comment on the subject, nonchalant yet delivered with the clear intention of closing this topic for good. There will be no more talk of butts. She turned her attention back to the intricate embroidery spread across her lap, a receiving blanket for the most recent grandchild. A new generation beckoned.

Said chafed, anyway, both about his queen-sized rear-end and his parent's disapproval. The fretting shaped habits: he concealed his curves beneath layers of fabric (as if he could; the ample mounds humping beneath the flapping tails will have no part of camouflage; that appendage will not be concealed). More efficiently, Said stashed his private thoughts and desires, relegating them to the realm of the voices within. The voices that drove him to Uncle's tonight.

None of the men notice Said, yet, or his quivering. Not even his butt. Notice comes slowly when a boy hides with such diligence. Still, Said carries a certain youthful appeal: an exotic, soft prettiness that fosters fantasies of plump submissiveness and quiet, thick acquiescence. Plus he earns bonus points for being fresh meat in this den of carnivores. He *will* eventually get noticed. But for now, although he has come on a mission, and swears to get to it soon enough, he needs this time to adjust. His senses are aflutter and before he joins the fray, they must be calmed.

If pressed, Said will lie. He will lay the blame for his shakes on the close call he had crossing Market Street on the walk here from the Muni station. After forty minutes of self- psyching on the journey from the conservative suburbs of Contra Costa County – "your butt isn't *that* big," the inward-facing voice had repeated, mantra-like – he was promptly distracted at the street-level window of Gold's Gym as he walked by. Only he wasn't trying to catch a glimpse of the muscle-heads hoisting grandiose poundage in the free-weight room, like the other passers-by. He wrenched his neck backwards to judge, via his reflection in the polished glass, how well he had managed to disguise the protrusion of his bottom.

"Not well at all," he mumbles to himself, tugging fruitlessly at the too-short tail of his Oxford.

The weight of Said's fabricated self-image crashed to the ground like a barbell that got away from the shaking arm trying to boost it. At the same moment, he stepped from the sidewalk directly into the path of a thundering streetcar. A horn blared and a small, feminine gasp escaped from his pink lips. Although he leapt backwards to the safety of the curb just in the nick of time, it was too late to salvage his self-composure.

Still, his persistent shuddering infers an upheaval that goes deeper than a simple near miss.

His escape to the Castro for a tryst induces this quake; the forgoing of his usual Saturday night spent sequestered in the bedroom he still occupies in his parent's home, door shut tight against his mother's overbearing supervision while he watches the latest from Netflix and shares a *chile verde* burrito with Diablo, the family cat. But even an insecure *chico* has hormones and tonight Said enters the race.

He stumbles blindly toward a life that he can't quite visualize, knowing only that skin-to-skin man-contact is a first step.

"*Voy al cine*," he lied to his mother, slipping away from the radar of her guardianship.

"*Voy al* dick," he might have said, had speaking the truth been possible.

But since it isn't, he arrives here in secret, under the dueling influences of Testosterone and Adrenalin.

Said hovers just inside the barroom until a duo of spit-slathered lovebirds shoves past him, grappling, walking, and kissing all at the same time with such focus that they don't even acknowledge the hard push that sends him careening to his left. He alights on the short end of the long bar where he stays, parked at the periphery of the party with his back to the wall.

"All the better to hide what isn't my best asset," justifies the internal dialogue.

The dim green flickering of the EXIT sign overhead provides a slim measure of comfort to Said; there is no telling when a quick escape may be necessary. Still, in dogged pursuit of both sexual release and socialization – the basal and the higher needs – he assumes a pose.

His right thumb parts the flaps of his shirttails and hooks into the front pocket of his jeans; the rest of his hand hangs provocatively near his crotch. Shoulders press back, chest pops out, eyes rove. He emulates his role models, the naked and narrow-waisted men displayed in the glossy magazines he hides from his mother's inquisition. Every cell of Said – even those comprising his rotund gluteus – climbs toward that pinnacle of studliness. But his impersonation falters: he stands too erect, as though the current of insecurity running through him carries a charge that stiffens his torso. His arms jut outward at an unnaturally stiff angle and his chin rides slightly too high. His eyes dart rather than rove. He strives for a look suggesting virility, but he achieves only over-compensation. And he squirms.

"What'll ya' have?" asks the boy behind the bar, a twenty-something artist-cum-bartender with tousled brown hair, tight jeans, and a sleeveless shirt. He speaks more in Said's general direction than at him, focusing instead on the dirty glasses he twists once on the upright, soapy bristle in the below-counter sink before swiping them briefly through the tepid rinse water and placing them on the "clean" rack.

"Vodka tonic," comes the muttered response.

The bartender wipes his brow with the back of his hand, and as he lifts his bare arm Said notices the patch of dark hair sprouting from the guy's pit, the tendrils trailing down his triceps to a moistened point. Said is nearly hairless, not bushy in even the usual places, and he swallows another wave of inadequacy as the bartender's thatch retreats beneath his lowered arm.

"What?" the bartender asks, finally lifting his gaze to his customer. "Hey, you new here? What's your name?"

"My name is Said, and I'll have a vodka tonic." The words are spoken with precision but the delivery remains timid, and they are lost in the ruckus swirling though the bar. "Please."

"OK, Ted, comin' up."

"SAY-eed. My name is Said."

"You Saudi or what?"

"No," Said responds with a sigh, "close, but no cigar. I'm Mexican."

Said has never grown easy with this line of questioning. His mother chose the name after hearing it in a late night movie. Full-bellied in the ninth month of her ninth pregnancy, she had risen from bed fighting a bout of indigestion stirred into froth by the kicking fetus. She liked the way the word rolled off her tongue, and so tagged her youngest child without thought to the confusion it would cause later in his life. Mexican, Saudi, Indian, Thai: to some, they are indistinguishable.

Said has argued with people about his name.

"Yes you are, you're Middle Eastern," some insist. "It's OK."

But the bartender doesn't argue; he isn't that interested.

"Mmmm," he merely grunts, turning to mix the drink. But what he finally pushes across the bar to Said is a gin and ginger ale, with a squished maraschino cherry slowly sinking to the bottom. Said pays, anyway, and tips, and then sips without complaint. He so rarely disobeys his mother's directive to avoid alcohol that the simple act of imbibing connotes sacrilege; confronting the inattentive barkeep stretches beyond Said's capacity for rebellion. Instead, he accepts what is handed to him, a just punishment for his intentions.

Detlef Von Steinle stands at the waist-high, circular tabletop smack in the center of Uncle's, his right hand casually curled around the green glass of his cold Heineken, his fingertips tapping to the music that blares from the overhead speakers. The beers arrive as if by magic, the empties whisked away and replaced by full bottles without his even asking. Detlef has slept with all of Uncle's bartenders at one time or another; he has slept with most of the men who patronize this dank watering hole. He lives up to a credo of living while the living is good. Even in his relative youth he has more notches on his belt than many, and yet he maintains an easy rapport with most of his conquests. Bartenders included. They remember what he drinks and they keep the Heinies coming.

Detlef stands here because he knows – this *is* his hangout – that this center-most table offers the best chance for garnering attention from the men who inhabit Uncle's. Not that he needs to worry about such; his blond-Adonis looks imply an all-American diet of grain-fed meat, fresh sweet corn, and whole milk, belying his solid German heritage (he was in truth reared on his mother's hand-crafted gnocchi and strudel). Whatever the diet, it worked, as the sum total of golden curls framing clear skin, wide-set blue eyes poised above a lantern-jaw, and broad shoulders tapering to a narrow waistline far out-scores the other numbers in this bar. Detlef doesn't need to pose. He naturally entices and he has never hesitated to take advantage of this lucky draw. Detlef has never wanted for attention.

So it is no surprise when a stranger sidles up his table.

"'Sup, handsome?" asks the stranger. "I'm Randy. Randy Bartlett."

"Hey man, how's it goin'?" Detlef answers. He auto-replies, more from force of habit than desire. It is a conditioned response, rote pleasantry stemming from a long history of tawdry positive reinforcement. He smiles on cue and the stranger interprets his slight participation as encouragement. Mr. Randy Bartlett embarks on a rapid, blurring monologue; he will not squander this good fortune with uncomfortable conversational pauses.

Against the backdrop of the numbing ramble of Mr. Bartlett's soliloquy, Detlef's own inner voice rings clear, bell-like: "The guy isn't quite butt-ugly," it allows. "In fact, he was probably a stud a hundred years ago."

Randy stands taller than the coveted hunk, and beefier, but not with the thick musculature of steak. His girth hints more of potatoes: a dollop of self-abuse spooned over a hefty portion of neglect. No regular sleep, pyramidal meal plans, nor exercise regime; just drink after drink after drink interspersed with fumbled huffing of poppers on the dance floor culminating in too many ambitious sex acts with more men than he can count.

The result? A fleshy triangle; a heavy apical midriff hanging from narrow, slanted shoulders.

"I like a stout man," Detlef's internal dialogue observes, with honesty. Given his preferences, he will pick someone with physical substance. "However," his rumination continues, "this one grew into a pear of a man."

Detlef amuses himself with the witticism of the pear-man's unfortunate but fitting family name until another surreptitious glance reveals a black leather belt cinching the pursuer's significant belly tight across the most bulbous part, overhung by the dimpled mass it strives to contain. No joke in that.

Pear-man blathers on, and in lieu of Detlef's standard modus operandi of taking on the fellow's fantasy purely for the sake of conquest, ending up (no pun intended) naked in the rumpled sheets of the distorted stranger's bed, he pauses. Occasionally even the fortunate, the genetically-blessed and sexually experimental, are tugged from beneath the warm blanket of attention and thrust buck-nekkid into the chilly air of reality. As difficult as habits of pleasure are to shake, of late a new hankering colors Detlef's inner pondering; an itch not easily scratched by the luck of good looks and the fixation of strangers. This thirst requires a different drink.

He has his mother to thank.

Flash back to Detlef's thirty-third birthday just last month. Mama Von Steinle hosted a party for him, inviting his innermost circle of man pals to join the family in the vintage Victorian above The Presidio on Lake Street. They celebrated the prodigal son with champagne, truffles, and song, but Mama struck a lingering chord when, in German-tinged but impeccably enunciated English, she issued a call to arms, an invitation for him to change his priorities. Not that Mama objected to his lifestyle; she and the senior Detlef (a software engineer lured into the lucrative service of the Silicon Valley) had emigrated from Amsterdam the year before their only child's birth, and along with the good Lenox china and Waterford crystal they imported a cultural acceptance of the range of human sexualities. Detlef-the-junior's sexual orientation was – *is* – not of concern to her. Her unease arises from her son's continued bachelorhood.

"You listen to me, *Bübchen*, it's all fine and dandy that you and your *reisigbündel* friends have had your fun drinking and whoring like a pack of she-wolves, but sooner or later you will need to settle down," she chided as Detlef and the gang prepared to shift the celebration to

Uncle's. "You're not getting any younger," she added, swatting the Belgian lace tablecloth in her hands at the American denim stretched across his perky bottom. He just laughed as he moved past her, ushering his friends out the door.

But her words stuck with him, and since then his inner voice increasingly directs him to search at Uncle's not so much for a roll, but a role: that of partner. Husband. Significant other. The plucky boy wants to get lucky for more than the night. He seeks the charm of a lifetime. Trouble is, the men at Uncle's aren't the stay-put sort. They have been around this block more than once and they can't stop circling. They are a hardened lot, jaded by a life spent maneuvering between the thrill of the adventure and the letdown of rejection. They are man-sharks who frenzy feed, yet no number of flesh-meals will satiate their appetites.

"These barracudas don't fit the bill," admits the inward-speaking voice, as Detlef eyes the motley collection. "Especially not pear-man," whose droning, non-stop prattle, the content of which Detlef would be hard-pressed to remember, serves only to further diminish his minimal attractiveness. Pear-man might suffice for an hour's play but Detlef fishes for a different species. His pining requires a special catch: a spawn that has not yet developed the hard shell mandated for survival in these predatory waters.

"I need a newbie," says the internal dialogue.

"Like that guy over there," Detlef says, aloud, noticing for the first time the youngster – Said – standing across the dusky room. Detlef surveys the uncomfortable pose, the fidgeting, and the timid sipping of the cocktail: all good signs. And it's just another benefit that he looks to be full-figured. For Detlef, a round ass sets the hook. He has a passion for some junk in the trunk; he's fond of the cushion. This one seems to offer a nicely filled-out resumé.

"What?" asks the pear-shaped man, but without pausing for a reply continues his one-sided dialogue, oblivious to the give-and-take concept of conversation. The syllables fall from his mouth and land, unheard, in the pile of noise in the room. Detlef pays no mind; he sees nothing but the dark-featured curvy boy across the room. The golden panther targets the grass-fattened *chivito*. The hunt begins.

Across the room, Said questions his decision to venture to the Castro. His anxiety grows in direct and inverse proportion to the shrinking of his commitment to this undertaking. He may have been better served by sticking (although not literally) to his nudie photo spreads and all-accepting right hand.

"Maybe," concludes his internal dialogue, "this was a mistake."

He studies the men congregated around him. He looks carefully at each specimen, panning from left to right, but he sees no indication of interest in him: not a nod nor a smile. Not even a casual but intentional self-caressing of the carefully-positioned bump straining the front of worn jeans.

Until his gaze lands on the striking blond fellow standing in the center of the room, staring.

"Staring at what?" asks Said's skittish inner voice.

The blond produces a smile that out-dazzles any tooth-whitening advertisement and imbues more mystique than all of the beefcake spreads tucked out of maternal sight between Said's mattresses. This smile is very nearly a laugh; mischievous, conspiratorial, direct.

"*Must* be someone behind me," warns the voice within, growing more critical as it feeds from the plentiful trough of doubt, nagging so loudly that Said has no choice but to listen. With what he intends to be a casual, dismissive move (but in truth, and consistent with his overall presentation, is more a reactive jerk), Said looks back to see who prompts the stranger's mirth.

Only no one loiters back there, just a floor-to-ceiling mirror that perfectly illuminates for all onlookers a larger-than-life reflection of his nether region, its expanse broadened not as much by the convex curvature of the flimsy and inexpertly-hung glass as by the fun-house distortion of his own self-perception.

"*Ay, dios mio!*" Said says out loud. "He's laughing at my ass."

He tosses his unfinished cocktail toward the bar top, sloshing the remains of the bitter concoction over the smudged surface. The lop-sided cherry scoots across the counter and disappears over the far edge of the bar. The bored bartender glances up in response to the clatter but makes no move to clean the spill, while Said turns on his heels and scampers through the passage below the green EXIT sign. Color him gone. He won't look back, he won't pass go. He doesn't even pause to blink after passing from the dark privacy of the tavern to the vigorous, neon- and halogen-lighted perpetual brightness of the street. He trots straight toward the train, hell bent on the safety of home (mindful, however, of oncoming streetcars). Diablo and a warm burrito wait, and at this juncture he craves that measure of reassurance.

Detlef watches the *hinter* of his dreams hustle what could have been the man of his dreams out of the bar. He makes no other move. A different man might run after the boy, but here's the sad truth: the backside of being god-like is that the beautiful become spoiled – why plant a garden when the farmers throw food at your feet? And having never grown a garden, Detlef can't even harness the plow. Watching the ass vanish is all he can muster. Still, his history doesn't include ditching and this quarry's sudden departure unsettles him. He lurches momentarily toward an abyss he has never faced. His golden aura tarnishes.

He sees his own reflection in the empty fun house mirror the young man left, and for the first time notices a slight wrinkling around the eyes, just the tiniest bulge of too many beers beneath the tightly-stretched tee shirt. "Damn, am I getting old?" the ever present internal voice asks. But Detlef quickly dismisses this line of thought. The ramifications are beyond him. His equilibrium may have been momentarily up-ended, but he teeters only briefly on the edge of the gaping pit of self-doubt. He moves quickly to regain his footing.

"So, Randy, right?" he says to pear-man, "you feeling randy?"

Pear-man replies by sliding the tip of his index finger, chilled from clutching his own bottle, along the top of the low-rise denims hugging Detlef's butt. His fingertip disappears into the downy cleft just below the fabric's edge.

"Mr. Bartlett, just like the pear," Detlef quips, "what do you say we make like fruits and peel outta here?"

GOOD WEED, BAD DEED

I was a late-bloomer as far as sex was concerned. At least compared to the other boys in my dusty little hometown in northern Wyoming in the mid-1970's. Most of them bragged about nailing some cheerleader by the time they were fifteen. Even by seventeen, the only nailing I did involved a hammer and wood. But I did like hearing their stories. The locker room talk was steamy.

Sure, I had dates. Plenty of dates. I was good-looking in a ruggedly handsome way. I had loads of wavy hair, sky-blue eyes, and nice muscles. I was lucky in the looks department. And the girls liked to give me attention, appreciating my sensitive and artistic nature as much as my physicality. It's just that when it came down to the cold facts, I got cold feet. Cramped up in the back seat of someone's mother's Chevrolet – an overheated nymphet wriggling beneath me with her mound of Venus thrust toward my hesitant member – I froze.

I knew I was supposed to slip a sweating palm beneath her bra cup or shove it under the elastic waistband of her panties, but I couldn't. I always found a reason to stop.

"Not here. I don't want it to be like this. Let's wait," I would whisper. What I really meant was, "not here, not you, I'm scared and I want to go home." Eventually I would extricate myself from the damp tangle of arms and legs and partially clothed torsos. After a moment to cool down, the girl usually found my reticence romantic. I was just happy it was over. Girls petrified me, and I didn't know what I was supposed to do.

Then Becky found me.

Back in 1976, in a one-light town in the middle of a huge nowhere, without a theater or club or even a late-night restaurant, a group of teenagers were forced to find their own means of entertainment. My friends and I turned to marijuana. Enter Hank and Becky.

They moved in from Oregon, kids and dog in tow. After an introduction through someone's older brother, Hank became our "source". He received shipments in the mail, usually in the form of a cute little stuffed animal, its cotton batting replaced with high grade Mexican weed. This was a decent second income for his family, and we provided him a good business: such good business that we ended up seeing a great deal of them. Eventually we all became friends. Their living room became our hangout. It didn't matter that they were in their thirties and we were in our teens. Ganja was the great equalizer. We passed the time rolling fat joints, eating junk food, and laughing. We were one big, high, happy family.

Hank was a huge man, unkempt, over six feet tall and burly, with hair and a beard like Grizzly Adams and arms bigger than my waist. He was loud and aggressive and ruled his house with an iron fist. Literally. His dog, his children, even his friends toed the line. Nobody wanted to incur Hank's wrath. Funny thing is, Becky might not have been as big or loud or aggressive, but she definitely schemed better. Becky didn't take crap. Everyone, including Hank, ended up following her lead. He had the cocksure bravado, but she ruled that roost like the clucking mother hen she was.

By no means a beauty – two children and lots of marijuana munchies had left a sag here and a bag there – Becky's infectious laugh and easy comic flair were her appeal. She was the jovial den mother for our troop of Rastafarian-wannabe scouts, a merry leader with an uncanny ability to get exactly what she wanted. We all loved Becky and the power of her wit, and where she ventured, our little band of misfits and outcasts followed: a string of hapless, stoned baby ducks. No one loved her more than I. In the midst of this spaced-out crush I gave up grappling with girls and devoted myself to spending time with Becky and her bong. I would have gone anywhere with her.

As it turned out I only had to go as far as Billings, one-hundred-and-change miles to the north. In this wide-open part of the country, this was the city. It was time to restock our pothead paraphernalia and Billings lay claim to the only headshop within driving distance. Becky arranged for the two of us to make the trip on everyone's behalf. I skipped my classes the day of our venture, dressed with care and an eye toward looking older, and we headed north to Montana in a blaze of smoke. Becky drove. I loved being with her as she guided us to the city;

I even liked the way her breasts jiggled when the car passed over bumps in the highway.

As night fell and we headed back to Wyoming, I was quiet. Shopping for the latest in dope accoutrement had been fun, but being with Becky was a schoolboy fantasy. I was reluctant to return her to Hank. When she suggested a detour through Yellowstone Park for a moonlight drive, I quickly agreed.

It was a warm autumn night. My new Fleetwood Mac cassette was terrific, the breeze was pine-scented, and the moon cast a gentle blue glow to the forest. The romance overpowered me. When Becky suggested that we stop to stargaze, I was only too willing. She climbed into the back seat – for a better view, of course – and I followed her without hesitation, pulled by the electric current between us.

As we spooned in the back seat, her ample bottom pressed against the crook of my torso, I found myself getting hard. I guess Becky found it, too. She flipped around, kissed me, and took off both our shirts in what seemed like one quick move. As she slid my hand over her maternal breast my palm wasn't sweating, and I didn't resist when she licked her way down my bare chest, unbuttoned my straining jeans, and took me in her mouth. Later, as she straddled my hips from above and aimed herself at my dick, her hippie skirt hiked up and my jeans pulled down, I had a sudden flash of understanding. Maybe it was her intensity, the way she took command without offering a chance for protest. This is why she and I had made this trip alone. This was her purpose. And I didn't care. At that moment I loved her more than anything.

After the initial wilderness devirginization she became insatiable, plotting ways for us to be alone. We would clandestinely drive to the country, rocking her car on some solitary farm road, or she would pick me up a discrete distance from the high school for my lunch break and take me to her house, her hand in my pants the entire distance. Creeping in the house to avoid being seen, she would toss me to the floor and ride me like a banshee for exactly 45 minutes, both of us with one ear cocked for sounds of Hank's unexpected return. I would leave her wet and asleep on her living room floor, running back to class five minutes late and flushed red.

A year passed and we were still secret lovers. I graduated from high school and took a job in one of the mines, putting off college because Becky asked me to stick around. I was working the swing shift, volunteering for the less desirable evening hours so that my days – when Hank was working – were free for frolicking. Over time Becky became more and more brazen, flicking her tongue against the back of my neck in their kitchen when Hank wasn't looking or groping me as we passed each other in their hallway. She was in her stride, but for me things were at a standstill. Gradually my days had settled into a numbing inertia that I couldn't explain. I worked, smoked pot, and put out for Becky as she arranged it. We professed our love for each other but I felt something was missing, and it felt like something important. I didn't know what it was, but even the sex lacked velocity. Sure, I was living every boy's fantasy but I resented the secrecy. I was reduced to a pat on the ass here, a quick cup of the balls there, a toss on the floor when time and opportunity permitted. I wanted something else, but I didn't know what. It was a push-pull situation. I loved the love, but hated being her meat. And I couldn't stop.

One afternoon as I lay naked on my back on her living room floor, Becky grinding on top while I followed with the appropriate motions from below, I noticed her youngest daughter had quietly slipped in and was watching us. She had sneaked home unannounced from a neighborhood friend's house. At six, she wasn't old enough to know exactly what was going on but she knew it wasn't right. She bolted. Becky didn't care; she wanted to finish.

That night when my shift ended and I walked through the moonlight to my car at the edge of the graveled parking lot, I really wasn't surprised to see Hank leaning against it, waiting for me. I may not have been world-wise in matters of sex and relationships, but after a year of hiding from this behemoth, I knew that things had come to a head. I had practiced for this moment. I was prepared. When I noticed that Hank was holding the biggest bone-handled hunting knife I had ever seen, my rehearsed speech about the love that Becky and I felt – the love that could never be denied – stuck solidly in my throat like a piece of dry bread. Before I could catch my breath, he began to speak. He didn't look at me; instead, he focused on cleaning the grit from beneath his fingernails with the tip of the blade.

"Do you think you're the only one? That she hasn't done this before? Do you think I didn't know?" Hank mumbled, as much to himself as to me. He continued, not waiting for a response. "It's always a boy like you, some kid she can boss around. Some skinny little sensitive kid who does exactly what she wants. Do you think she really loves you?" The polished metal of the blade glistened delicately in the moonlight, and I thought it best not to speak.

He looked at me and continued, slowly. "She likes boys, sissy boys, and you're just the latest. Why do you think we left Oregon? Goddam it! I tell her every time that she can't keep doing this." He turned his head and spat at the ground, as if clearing his throat would help clear his mind. I remained silent. We both stared at the dirt-flecked puddle of spittle as he spoke.

"She loves me, you know. She doesn't love you, and she didn't love any of them. She just likes a young dick. She's always going to be with me, and I'm always going to be with her. We are a family." He looked at me with a steely glare, opened the door and motioned for me to get in, gesturing to the empty driver's seat with the knifepoint. He did not break eye contact. As I slid past his imposing bulk, I noticed that I really was much shorter and smaller than he. Oh my God, I was a skinny kid! I sat behind the wheel and he closed the door behind me. He leaned through the open window, his huge frame filling the space.

"Only I'm not leaving this time," he said, nearly whispering. "You are."

With an eerie calm and more authority than I had ever heard before, he told me that I had to be gone by morning. I couldn't say good-bye to Becky; I wasn't to tell anyone about our conversation. As if to illustrate the seriousness of his instructions, Hank absent-mindedly made a series of cuts in the rubber window moulding as he spoke. The flawlessly sharpened knife effortlessly sliced through the fleshy material. I watched in awe, barely hearing him yet completely understanding every word. Then he walked back to his old truck and waited for me to drive away. He followed me out of the parking lot, so close behind that in my rearview mirror I could see the glint of the knife he continued to hold in his hand as he drove. He followed me all the way home.

Through the early morning hours, as I packed what I would be taking on the road, Hank's words came back to haunt me. "Skinny, sensitive kid. Sissy boy." It was a mantra that repeated as I drove away from the sleeping town at sunrise. "Skinny, sensitive kid. Sissy boy."

The remarkable thing is, I wasn't sad. Instead, I felt renewed, as if breaking the surface for fresh air after being submerged far too long in a murky depth. Here in the bright morning sunlight, the fresh country air fluffing my hair through the open car window, both the boy having sex with an older woman on the floor of her living room and the "other man" being threatened in a dark parking lot seemed distant and remote. Leaving the only life I had known, I drove alone, without a destination but for the first time in my own direction. Unfettered by expectation, I began to see myself with clarity, not in a bright and sudden flash of insight but incrementally, a gradual claiming of the pieces of myself I found along that highway. My sensitivity was both salvation and strength. As the miles ticked by, I began to understand that I was gay, and I knew that I had to move forward to embrace that destiny.

Life opened for me that morning. I felt like I had been given a gift and I was grateful. I wanted to turn the car around and drive straight back to Hank and Becky's, to thank them for setting me free. I wanted to reassure them that they would be OK, that I would be OK. As I searched for a wide spot in the highway to make a U-turn, my hand came to rest on the jagged edges of the cuts in the window moulding. Tracing the sharp outlines with one finger, I realized that turning around wasn't such a great idea. Let them fend for themselves. I pointed the car south and pushed the gas pedal. And I haven't looked back.

SLICES

The evening before Thanksgiving, the city is dark. In his bright studio apartment's kitchen, Jesús Jimenez-Callaghan attacks pecans with a large knife. His drooping tangerine and turquoise boxers are smudged with flour. He chats with Carlos, who reclines on the adjacent Queen-sized bed. Carlos wears only a gingham apron and a chef's hat.

Jesús reads Betty Crocker's Sugar-Crusted Pecan Pie recipe aloud for a fifth time and then lifts a sample from each of the two piles he has hacked to pieces. The one in his left hand is miniscule; the right, bigger.

"Hey, Carlito, which of these would you say is chopped?" There is no answer. Jesús mixes both piles into one.

He believes that one day he will prepare a glorious meal and his family will be transformed by the dishes he has offered. Peace will settle over them like a flower picker's poncho in a Diego Rivera painting.

He does not see his inability to cook as an obstacle.

A few miles away his adoptive grandmother, Old Mrs. Callaghan, dices fresh flat leaf parsley for oyster stuffing, her Thanksgiving dinner specialty. The green scent of the herb reminds her of a time some twenty years earlier when Jesús refused to eat the corned beef and cabbage she had stewed all day for the family's Good Friday dinner. He was only five, and the powerful smell of that dish offended his naïve nose. He stubbornly shook his head side-to-side while Old Mrs. Callaghan just as stubbornly chased his mouth with a spoon.

"Take a bite."

"No."

"One little bite."

"No."

"You will sit here until you eat some."

Jesús scowled from the powder blue dinette chair for three hours, clutching his teddy bear in defiant little fingers. By the time a defeated Old Mrs. Callaghan dismissed him with a sweep of her hand, chick-a-dees and goldfinches had begun their twilight songs in the backyard roses. She dumped the coagulated food in the silver kitchen pail.

Later she watched as Jesús' mother fixed him packaged tortillas and canned refried beans.

Old Mrs. Callaghan vowed never to teach either to cook.

Colin Callaghan pours himself a whisky and watches his elderly mother dice the parsley. Something in the way she deftly turns the blade scares him, and when he is scared he tends to remember when his father died. Colin was two. His mother, he recollects, used to delight in telling Colin that his father had been found sprawled on the dining room floor.

"Like a boar laid out for skinning," she's told him over the years, pointing a harsh finger or a stirring spoon or, yes, a boning knife, "right there on the cold marble tiles." This information highly disturbed the fatherless boy. It still does.

Old Mrs. Callaghan also told Colin that directly after his father died she emptied two-and-a-half fifths of Irish whiskey down the toilet. Then she prayed.

MariaElena Jimenez-Callaghan picks through black beans. She will cook them in her special bean pot for the Thanksgiving dinner. She has sifted through beans so many times over the course of her 45 years that her fingers complete the task without thought, knowing by touch whether it's good bean or bad bean or rock. Her unencumbered mind reminisces about how she became a part of this family.

The twenty-year-old Mexican national learned she was pregnant with Jesús on a Saturday. That Monday, accompanied only by the fetus and the long shadow she cast in the midnight moonlight, she sprinted across a wide-open U.S. border. Once on the American side she didn't stop running until she landed in a maid's uniform in the Maryland suburbs of Washington. The baby's father, simple and fixated on doing what he'd been taught was right, and in love with MariaElena, followed her faint trail.

"*¿Quieres casarte conmigo?*" he proposed when he found her.

"Hell no," she answered. If she took a husband, he would be a citizenship-providing American with sufficient resources.

In a tequila-fueled attempt to prove his spousal worthiness, the rejected suitor robbed the SunTrust bank on DuPont Circle using a water pistol and broken English. He was sentenced four months later.

On the day of Jesús' birth he mailed a prison-commissary teddy bear, and two weeks after that, mistaken in a dark corridor for a different brown-skinned inmate, he was stabbed to death with the crudely-sharpened leg bone of a turkey.

As a Training Associate in the International University's Human Resources Department, Jesús could trade up from this shabby studio apartment on 13th Street, with its listing avocado green range and mismatched harvest gold refrigerator. But he stays because everything he needs is within easy reach. He cooks in his underwear because the kitchen and bedroom are one and the same.

"Why would anyone want more rooms than they can reasonably occupy?" he asks Carlos as he lightly beats three eggs for the pie's filling.

Colin ignores his mother's sideways sneer as he pours a second whiskey. He believes he came by his taste for the drink naturally.

"I'm Irish, for Christ's sake."

He takes his poison from a cut crystal old-fashioned glass. He adds a solitary ice cube. As he often does, Colin holds the drink up to the back parlor window overlooking the rose garden; he appreciates the way the yard light plays through the amber liquid and refracts in the glass' angles. The flowers and thorns glow golden through the spirits. Colin dangles the glass between two calloused fingers aligned so as not to block a single beam of light. He sniffs the drink's caustic vapors and then slugs it back in one gulp. He pours another.

MariaElena dumps the cleaned beans into the cast iron pot and covers them with water. She adds salt and pepper, onions, celery, salt pork, garlic, and a bay leaf. She reaches around her mother-in-law to pull the ingredients from their storage.

"Good thing Jesús is making his pie at his place," she says. "It's crowded here." She says this even though she misses her son's warmth in this drafty old house. Until he moved out two years ago, they hadn't been apart since she'd birthed the howling little U.S. citizen at Brigham Women's Hospital.

For the first year of Jesús' life, between maid gigs and breastfeeding, MariaElena halfheartedly studied for the naturalization exam. She failed. Twice. After that she set her sights on the passive Irishman she met on a Metrorail platform one lip-chapping winter day. She and Colin were married late the following summer – over his mother's objections.

MariaElena turns the flame under the bean pot to high and stirs it. The hard beans rattle like river gravel across the pan's metal bottom.

MariaElena's mother, *Abeula* Jimenez, died when Jesús was ten. MariaElena and Jesús returned to *el Estado Chihuahua y la Cuidad Asencion en Mexico* to pack up *Abeula's* belongings. In the far back closet of the low-slung white adobe house they found two boxes of carefully wrapped *Nahua* iconography and texts, including rare *primitivo* sacrifice and cannibalism implements. Back in Maryland, as they unpacked the evidence of Jesús' other grandmother, Colin insisted that MariaElena send the iconography – anonymously and with no return address – to the National Museum of Mexican Art in Chicago.

"I'm telling you both; don't mention this to my mother – ever. This would be the last straw."

MariaElena curses in Spanish as the bean pot boils over with a loud hiss. Her fingers tingle crimson as she turns down the flame, but their warmth is not the result of the cooking heat. Like a volcano, malcontent simmers below her surface and at times her hands pang with longing. She has always known that one day she will erupt, and she is alternately fearful and welcoming of this prospect. Sometimes it takes all the grit she can muster to keep her hands from exploding into a million bits of shrapnel.

Old Mrs. Callaghan minces Chesapeake Bay oysters and adds them to the stuffing mixture. Her Irish in-laws had been disgusted when she'd made this dish for them during an American visit years ago; in Irish culinary norms, oyster stuffing was a slap across the shamrocks. But then, there had always been the impulse to slap between these in-laws.

Colin's father keeled over from a heart attack that had paddled toward him from the deep end of a whiskey pool for years. Upon hearing the news, his Irish sister demanded that the body be returned to Dublin. She wanted a proper burial in the family plot. The ensuing battle between the Irish and the American women became so heated that in a fit to resolve it, Old Mrs. Callaghan had her husband's remains cremated. She sent half the ashes to her sister-in-law, secured in a yellow and black Carhartt steel-toed boot box.

Colin watches MariaElena stir the beans. She is still lithe and nimble, he notes, still attractive at her age.

She was the first person he ever loved, including his mother.

"Who could love a mother like that?" he's asked Father O'Brien in the confession booth at St. Augustine. Father O'Brien advised patience.

Colin fell in love with MariaElena because she was lost when they met. Feeling disoriented himself, he'd appreciated the metaphor.

"Which way to Shady Grove," she'd asked?

Straight through my heart, was his first thought.

That was long ago. That train has left the station, and now they are two strangers standing on this platform. Waiting.

Jesús is the only person Colin still loves. He doesn't even care that he's turned up gay. He is in fact in many ways envious of Jesús' charmed life.

Colin regrets that he never went to college; instead, he followed his dead father's trail to become a Metrorail track repairman. He is envious of Jesús and his air-conditioned office job. He is envious of the Brooks Brothers wingtips that Jesús wears. Colin wears Carhartt steel toes over his wide, flat feet, just like his father did. He wishes they were steel heart guards; he is fully aware that in this house, hearts are in considerably more danger than toes.

Colin leaves the women in the kitchen and wanders back to the window overlooking the roses. The half of the dead Mr. Callaghan's ashes that were not returned to Dublin are sealed in that elaborate concrete urn jutting above the small goldfish pond. It has always been Colin's duty to feed the goldfish and tend the roses; to cultivate the soil in spring, to trim the spent flowers and straggling stems, to rinse the foliage with tepid water and Ivory dish soap at first appearance of aphids or black spot or leaf rust.

When he came in from an afternoon with the roses and his father, Old Mrs. Callaghan soaked Colin's blistered hands in more tepid water and Ivory dish soap. This softened the thorns he had collected, and then she plucked them with golden tweezers.

The one thing MariaElena loves about this house is that pond in the back yard. She sits among the roses in the humid summer afternoons and pretends to read. Instead, she watches the fish endlessly circle their tiny world, always moving but never going anywhere. From her seat on the short prickly grass she sometimes sees her husband at the window watching through his glass of yellow whiskey. He's like the fish, she thinks, circling his enclosure.

"Oh, *¡Dios mío!* but it's my cage, too," she whispers to herself.

On the day after his mother is buried, Colin plans to send the urn of ashes to Dublin and turn under the roses. He'll install a shallow pool and he'll circle it on a pale yellow floater. He'll drink to his father, whole again in Ireland.

Jesús lines the pie plate with the crumbling pastry that won't hold together. Before adding the nuts, he repairs as best he can the jagged rips across the crust's bottom. Then he crimps the edges exactly as illustrated by Betty Crocker. It looks professional, almost as good as his grandmother's. When he pours the custard mixture over the nuts a large dollop splashes onto his bare foot.

Jesús says his flat, brown feet are embarrassing. When young, his mother tickled them with her fingernails, called them *patas* (paws, like dogs). He covets his Grandma Callaghan's pink feet, still strong at her age. Those feet were made for marching, for standing firm.

Jesús confessed to Old Mrs. Callaghan in Wal-Mart two years ago. She was wandering aisle to aisle, searching for Ivory dish soap, when she found him holding up two different doll's dresses, comparing fabrics.

"Jesús , what are you doing?"

"Grandma, I'm gay."

Old Mrs. Callaghan looked away. "Where's the soap?"

She says she follows her church's teaching: hate the sin, love the sinner. But in practice she denies both.

Jesús places the assembled pie on the oven rack and sets the timer. "Viola!" he says to Carlos with an exaggerated gesture.

At 25, Jesús continues to sleep with, and talk to, this crusty teddy bear named Carlos that his father sent so many years ago. He also has hidden in a box under his bed an assortment of doll's dresses and hats that Carlos wears, depending on Jesús' mood. This includes a full leather dominatrix outfit. Jesús hasn't told anyone about the bear's clothing, especially since Carlos occasionally wears the child's burial dress secretly pilfered from *Abeula* Jimenez's hidden iconography. Jesús believes when the bear wears it, *Abeula* watches him – with glee – from her *Nahua* afterlife.

"Bedtime," Old Mrs. Callaghan decrees as she blankets the readied turkey with aluminum foil. MariaElena scrubs the last of the scorched beans from the stove top.

"Bedtime," Old Mrs. Callaghan repeats.

Colin and MariaElena were married 23 years ago at the Crofton Justice of the Peace's office. He was 26, and still a virgin. A two-year old Jesús was the best man. Old Mrs. Callaghan was not in attendance.

"I do."

"Yes, I do, too."

After the wedding, in the purple light of the hazy summer dusk, Colin brought the new Mrs. Callaghan and Jesús to the rose garden and introduced them to his father. Beneath the pink scent of American Beauties, the boy lay on his stomach and twiddled his fingers in the pond. When the hungry goldfish suckled them, he giggled. Colin thought it the most beautiful sound he'd ever heard.

Old Mrs. Callaghan watched them from the back porch, her bony fingers flying along the rosary beads in a manic rhythm. She crossed her arms and looked skyward.

"Bedtime," she'd announced that night, too.

They all went to their separate rooms.

Two days after her son's wedding, Old Mrs. Callaghan kidnapped Jesús. She smuggled the toddler to St. Augustine for a proper Catholic baptism, dressed him in the same white lace christening dress that Colin had worn for his baptism.

When Father O'Brien dribbled the holy water over Jesús' forehead, drops pooled in his eyes. He cried and squirmed.

Old Mrs. Callaghan held him still with sturdy hands. "You're in for a surprise if you think this is the worst things will get, Jesús – now hush."

Thanksgiving morning. Early, no sign of sunrise yet. Old Mrs. Callaghan struggles in her feather bed, confused, suffering with visions. This dream feels real to her, and not. In it, she hobbles for miles over a rough, tree-studded landscape, but she knows not where she is going. She knows only that she has to pee, and the only restroom she finds, which she stumbles upon over and over again, as though she is circling within her dream, is a men's room. It is buried underground and guarded over by scantily-clad men performing acrobatic tricks among the trees. Although none admit it, she knows they are homos.

"Come," they sing in tinsel voices. Their minted breath cools her flushed face. "We're your homo angels."

She barricades herself in a stall to do her business and when she ascends from the underground bathroom bunker a storm has boiled up; a thick cloud climbs the hillside toward her and the acrobats. It is like a black widow crawling up a child's chiffon dress – wisped appendages reach from the vaporous body, pull at the trees and hills and hoist the menace ever closer. They huddle and just as the spider-cloud envelopes them, she awakes.

Unfortunately, she has peed her bed.

Down the hall, MariaElena dresses for Thanksgiving Day. As a last touch, she hangs a tiny, brightly-colored folk art hummingbird pendant against her breastbone. This was a gift mailed stateside from her mother to honor the birth of Jesús. *Doña* Jimenez told MariaElena that she was like a hummingbird: beautiful, restless, necessary.

The first time she heard this, Old Mrs. Callaghan laughed.

"You're more like a mockingbird," she said to MariaElena. "You're always squawking, always imitating something you're not."

MariaElena swore back under her breath – in Spanish. She had refused to teach Jesús the language – she didn't want him to seem an outsider in his culture. She, however, easily resorts to it, especially when angry with her mother-in-law. Like then.

"I know you're saying something mean," Mrs. Callaghan accused from her lime green recliner. Her ankles were elevated, bound in flesh-tone compression stockings. MariaElena thought she was like an old coyote: nearsighted and lame but still able to hear a twig break across the forest.

"*Callarse, bruja!*" MariaElena whispered. She smiled sweetly through the sulfuric words.

Old Mrs. Callaghan changes her soiled bed linens and smuggles the wet sheets to the laundry room like a new bride embarrassed by the wedding night stains. She was flirting with spinsterhood herself, also still a virgin, on the rain-soaked spring day when she married the older Mr. Callaghan. On their wedding night, sodden from the celebratory drink, he didn't wash her softly with tender kisses. He shoved her to the bed and ran his workman's hands along her body. And then he had his way. His whiskey breath dribbled over her until finally he moaned and shuddered. The new Mrs. Callaghan refused to cry – this was her wifely duty – but every time he came to her afterwards, all she remembered was that night and his smell.

After Colin was born, he stopped coming to her.

Mid-afternoon now. A brilliant autumn sun filters red through the changing leaves of the maple tree in the front yard. For their Thanksgiving dinner, Colin removes the extension slat from the family's antique oak dining table. There are only the four of them, after all. Old Mrs. Callaghan palms an Irish lace tablecloth smooth and places four settings of her best Waterford china. Colin adds three cut crystal wine glasses and one old-fashioned glass. MariaElena contributes an oversized centerpiece of colorful handmade Mexican paper flowers.

"Let's do this," Colin says. He fills his glass with whiskey.

They dine family style. There is Old Mrs. Callaghan's roast turkey with oyster stuffing, MariaElena's black beans and rice, new potatoes (Mrs. Callaghan, in a begrudged nod to the Irish), cornbread (MariaElena), and Brussels sprouts (no one claims these). There is also a fresh salad with sliced avocados, and spotlighted in the wings is Jesús' pecan pie, beautiful with perfectly crimped golden pastry encircling a crunchy top of sugared pecans.

After the meal, Old Mrs. Callaghan ceremoniously slices the centerfold pie with a serrated silver knife while Jesús stands ready with the matching pie server. But the sugared pecan crust sinks into a molten center. The pie, through no obvious fault of Jesús' but obviously through some neglect or ignorance or mishandling, has not solidified. An unforgiving silence settles over the room.

"It's OK, son," Colin eventually says, "we're OK without dessert, anyway". He rises and plods to the liquor cabinet, his stocking feet thunk-thunk-thunking on the wide planks of the yellow pine floor. He pours a short glass of whiskey which he carries to the back parlor window. In his mind he redraws the dimensions of the floating pool.

MariaElena watches him, and then glances at her son, who in this moment of despair looks exactly like his father did when MariaElena announced he hadn't enough *dinero* to buy her hand in marriage. She looks to her mother-in-law who has one crooked finger stuck in the liquid pie filling but stares vacantly at the faded plaster ceiling. The familiar crimson burning settles in MariaElena's fingers, and her left hand caresses the carving knife Colin used to hack off the turkey's legs and reduce its breasts to slices. Her gold wedding band clinks against the forged silver blade.

"You know, Jesús, my first pie didn't work, either," Mrs. Callaghan announces, looking from face to face.

She speaks quietly, almost a whisper, and her unusual tone is as warm as fresh baked Tollhouse cookies. In her mind she has seen nearly-naked acrobats cavorting on the low horizontal branches of a lost forest; she has sought refuge from the cold downdraft of an impending thunderstorm, seen a hillside eaten alive by a living cloud. She has awakened in a humiliating puddle of lukewarm urine, only to discover that it has softened a lifetime's accumulation of thorns.

She licks her finger. "It's soup. It's lovely pecan soup. MariaElena, get some bowls – and not those tacky ones from your mother's house. Colin, get the whipped cream. Hurry now."

MariaElena lays down the carving knife, and Colin abandons his glass of whiskey. They both follow the orders as barked. Old Mrs. Callaghan's crepe-skinned hand reaches across the lace tablecloth and finds the hand of Jesús under the gaudy paper flowers. Her bony pink fingers encircle, embrace, his short brown ones.

"Cooking is from the heart, Jesús," Old Mrs. Callaghan continues. "It's science mixed with love flowing from your heart through your hands to the food. I learned from my mother, but," she shoots a mean eye toward MariaElena, "I wouldn't expect that in your case. Come by tomorrow, we'll work on making pies. But right now, let's have soup."

THE RAPTURE

Hey gurrrl, it's Jesus, where you at? Thank God you picked up 'cause I gotta tell you what happened Sunday night. Yeah I sound different, who wouldn't? Things is different for this boy. I'm in love. Hear me? *Love*. Listen 'a this, it's real.

So Sunday me and Shiva – you remember her, that big ole drag queen thang who wears the jewel in her navel? – Sunday night me and Shiva decide to go to The Sanctuary Club. Now I wasn't looking for nothing, mind you, 'cause you know how I been holed up lately, a real sad sack since that whole thing with Judas calling me out in front of everybody and everything. Two-faced jerk. I never felt so betrayed as I did at that last supper with him and all those guys and since then I just haven't felt like going out. I only went Sunday 'cause Shiva had a bad day, what with that hellion brat of hers, Vishnu, destroying the entire house. He set the drapes on fire. Did she tell you? Anyways, about nine o'clock or so, Shiva calls me at my parents' house and says she's gotta get out.

Yeah, yeah, I been staying there, staying in the basement. It's like a grave down there, a cave with no light and no air but it was kinda fitting my mood. I was feeling bleak 'cause on top of everything else I got fired from the Catholic Charities Petting Zoo. Pure jealousy: the animals liked me better than the other keepers. I can't help it; I just have a way with 'em. That dumb old Simon tried for three days to get the sheep to follow him, but every time I came around they all ran over to me. Baa baa baa...all running toward me like I was the good shepherd, leaving him standing there with his hands full of hay. He complained, said I didn't pull my weight when it was time to clean the manger. I tried to tell Father Francis that it wasn't my fault; that Simon Magus was just full o' sour grapes but Simon's been there since the zoo's creation and I was just the new guy so I got let go. Anyways, so I had to give up my little hole-in-the-wall apartment and move back to Mom and Joe's basement. Can you believe it? I swear, though, I'm about to rise up from that tomb. I have to git up outta there 'cause, honey, I'm in love.

So anyways, me and Shiva show up at Sanctuary and we head to the upstairs bar, you know, that one with the dance floor. Shiva asks me if I wanna little sumpin-sumpin to set the mood cause you know Shiva, she's all about the mood. But I tell her I don't need nothing cause DJ Buddha's got the place zen rockin', man. He's playing some tribal house fusion mix that's pure enlightenment. I says to Shiva *I don't need nothing, gurrrl, this music's doing it all for me.*

So we's dancing, me and Shiva, and just feeling the beats and it's all good until that creep Lucifer starts rubbing all over Shiva. You know Lucifer? Seems like that guy's everywhere. Everywhere I turn, there's Lucifer. Sure don't know his story. But that night he starts telling Shiva how if she just lets him have her goodies he's gonna keep her happy forever and she'll never want for nothing. *Never want for nothing* he keeps saying over and over again, rubbing on her butt like she's digging it or something only I can tell, she's not havin' it. Shiva, she can do way better than that creep. But he's rubbing all over her and she's tryna get away and finally she says to me *Jesus, we gotta get away from him or it's gonna get ugly. Come on, let's go downstairs.*

So we ditch Lucifer and go downstairs to that little alley, you know, that patio between the front bar and the back room where the dick dancers swing their stuff. We're standing there and the summer night air feels real nice 'cause me and Shiva, we worked up a sweat dancing and running away from Lucifer. So we's just standing there minding our own business and dissin' on all the peeps who's walking by when I saw him. Man, I saw him and I'm in love.

He was standing in that one corner, the dark one by the door where the hustlers give lap dances. He didn't look like he wanted a lap dance. Didn't look like he needed one. Looked like he needed me but he didn't know it yet. So he's standing there all six feet tall and dark curly hair and dark sexy eyes and dark stubble, just watching peeps like I was, only he isn't watching me. So I'm tossing my hair around – what you say? Yeah, I know that's cheap but sometimes these guys like my hair. They like long hair and a soft beard and linen pants and sandals. A little hippie-dippy freak gonna catch some guys for sures.

So we's standing there, me and Shiva, and I'm all tryna get this guy's attention, and who should walk up to him but Zeus. Yeah, that's right, Zeus, that big ole horndog dancer with the thunderbolt tattoo on his thigh. And I can tell, he wantsa give more that a lap dance.

That's right, that ho was tryna cock block me, and I wasn't feeling it at all. I was mad, but I was nervous, too. I mean, the king of the dancers slides up to my man, now what's a little pacifist like me supposed to do? So there I am, tryna come up with my next move, and Zeus is starting his rub on this guy, and I look up and the guy is staring right over Zeus' shoulder at me. At me! And I'm thanking God and tryna look pretty at the same time.

So this guy pushes Zeus away and walks over to me and Shiva. Pushes Zeus and his oak-sized piece away, to come to me. Don't need nothing more than that 'cause my night's made right there but then this guy just walks up and says *'sup boy? My name's Mohammed, you can call me Moe.*

Moe, Moe, Moe, I'm thinking, give me Moe. I'm seeing myself writing Mrs. Moe all over everything I own, I'm seeing myself telling him right then and there that I love him and that's that. But I don't, I just say *Jesus - my name's Jesus, I'm just dancing with my friend Shiva* but when I turn to introduce them, Shiva's gone. Never saw her again the whole night. Bitch knows when to disappear.

So me and Moe's just standing there shooting the breeze and we end up talking about everything. He's telling me how he lives with his dad, Abraham, so I tell him about living in my parents' basement and all kinds of stuff and I mean, I'm telling this guy things I never told no one. That's right, not even you. I'm telling him how Mom got

61

knocked up wit' me and the guy disappeared but Joe came along and he took us in and raised me like a son and I'm just making all this noise like this guy cares and he's making his noise right back at me and then I think *Dang, this guy does care.*

Gurrrl, I'm saying I'm in love. That's all I'm saying.

So then we start getting a little close and he's touching my back and his fingers are running under the linen and I can't help myself but I gotta feel his chest so I do and, honey, I ain't disappointed. The man's built like Plymouth Rock. Then he kisses me and I'm telling you his stubble is hella sexy on my lips and I'm like warm salt water, all kinda heavy and liquid and melting right into this guy and next thing he says *let's go somewhere a little more private.*

Yeah, dude, that's what he says. So, OK, problem. We's both staying with our parents. I mean, Mom and Joe are real supportive and they don't care who I play around with but they don't want no strangers in their house, and Moe says his dad don't really know too much and will pitch a hissy-fit if he brings some long-haired hippy chile into the apartment. Bottom line's nobody's got nothing private. So I'm all like *OK, let's at least take a walk out on the beach and make out for a while.*

So we walk out to the beach and we're tryna find a place that's kinda hidden and finally Moe finds a spot that's pretty much outta sight, just off the beach walk but behind some rushes, and the sand feels soft and clean so we lay down. First thing we see a star in the sky, brightest star I've ever seen. So Moe tells me to make a wish and I do and he wants to know what it is but I don't tell him 'cause it's him I'm wishing for. So he starts tickling me and, honey, that's when the going gets good. I'm telling you. We're kissing and rubbing and touching and kissing some more and next thing you know my linen pants are in the bushes and so are Moe's jeans. And me and Moe's rolling buck nekkid in the sand like driftwood and I can tell he wants to go for it but then I realize my butt crack is full of sand. I think, *this can't work.*

Moe, I say, *this ain't gonna happen here. I like you, a lot, and I really wanna mess around and more but this just ain't working.* And Moe looks a little sad but he gets over it kinda quick and then he makes me promise that I ain't shining him on. *You aren't shining me on?* he asks, real serious. *I've been shined on before and I don't like it.* So I kiss him, just as serious, and we lay back down and we just keep talking and kissing, kissing and talking all night long, naked on the sand under the full summer moon with the breeze rustling the rushes and the waves lapping the shore just like our tongues lapping each other.

I know, gurrrl, it's getting kinda hot over here, too.

So then just when the sun's coming up, this lesbian rent-a-cop comes along – Sergeant Helios, her name badge says – and busts us. *You boys better git up and git dressed and git home,* she says, all butch and mean like she's got the power, like she made the sun come up. Thing is, the sun was coming up and we was pretty much naked so we did what she said. So I'm shaking about a gallon of sand out of my butt and it's trickling down my pants and out the cuff and Moe's doing the same with his jeans and we're all quiet like we don't really know how to say good-bye, only I know I feel like something in the world's changed, like oil and water can mix or dogs and cats can be friends. I just feel bright and big, full of potential like the sun coming up over the

Atlantic, man. I feel like some kinda divine something's opened up for me. And then Moe says to me, he says *I know it's only the first time we've been together and I'm probably breaking all the rules of hookups and dating* – he says dating, like we's already an item and then without missing a beat he keeps right on talking – *but I think I love you and I know I want to spend more time with you.* Then this angel tells me he don't wanna lose me.

I know, boyfriend, you better sit down 'cause I could hardly believe it myself. Gurrrl, this man is saying this to me. I feel like the luckiest boy on the planet. I feel like karma and fate and destiny have all rolled up to my feet in one beautiful package and I think to myself, *Moe, that ain't gonna happen, you stuck with me now.* So that's what I tell Moe. I tell him that it ain't gonna happen, that he ain't gonna lose me and that we're gonna have lots of nights and mornings and days and weeks and months and years.

Then Moe tells me he loves me again and he starts to walk away, only I remember that nobody's got anybody's digits and if I let him walk away, he's gonna lose me. And I'm gonna lose him. So I tell Moe to wait while I go find Sergeant Helios down the walk and I borrow her pen and I make Moe write down his number on the only scrap of paper I can find in the sand. You know what it was? A playing card, the two of hearts. No joke, man, the dang two of hearts.

And then I watch as Moe disappears in the rushes around a curve in the sidewalk and it looks like's he's floating down a river and just floats around the bend outta sight.

Honey, I know, you ain't gotta tell me. Right when I didn't think it was possible. What's that? Oh, yeah, gurrrl, I forgotta tell you,

I got a job doing construction over at the new Nazareth Retirement Center. I'm gonna be a carpenter! My first pay check is next Friday and I already made plans to get my apartment back and then that Moe gonna catch hell. I'm telling you, I'm gonna wear that man out.

So what you been up to, gurrrl? Tell me everything.

TALKING THROUGH THE NOISE

It's no secret: fags are noisy. I am allowed to say that without repercussion because I am one (A fag. A noisy fag.) If you've ever attended a happy hour function at your local gay bar – say, a Bear Happy Hour at your local dance club – you will have to agree. Cram five or six hundred hirsute sissies into one large room, stir in copious amounts of cheap beer and even cheaper vodka, sprinkle with drama, angst, and showmanship, then overlay the whole production with Lady Gaga screaming at an eardrum-perforating decibel count and you have produced a noise level comparable to two or three medium-sized atomic bombs blowing up simultaneously.

It matters not what each individual flannel- or too-small-tee-clad homo's agenda is – whether he is trying to attract the attention of the stud across the dance floor or arguing with his best friend about who slept with whose intended or embellishing a story about what shenanigans occurred at the local bath house last weekend – 97% of the conversations are 98% too loud and 99% ignored or interrupted. And they are 100% occurring at the same time. We fags are boisterous, rambunctious, rowdy, and self-serving. We yell and shriek and squeal more than straight folk, more than lesbians. More, even, than small, spoiled children.

There is very little quiet time in the social life of the urban gay, and zero time for thoughtful exchange. And I am possibly the worst offender in this world of offense. I am the loudest, most distracted, most interrupting gay of all.

Enter Sweet Sammy, a man I have had the pleasure of befriending. Sweet and deaf. Sweet Sammy has introduced me to a whole new world: a world of talking through the noise.

When I spend time with Sammy, we communicate primarily using American Sign Language (ASL). My proficiency level is rudimentary at best, but improving. When my tenuous grasp of ASL fails – I become incompetent after a few drinks or when I am sleep-deprived or emotionally charged – we write notes back and forth in a little notebook Sammy always keeps handy. I feel slightly illicit writing the notes, like bored kids in a high school history class.

Something unexpected and charming happens when I chat with Sammy in ASL. It feels like the world's overwhelming cacophony fades away, and time slows down. The quiet and the perceptual deceleration are neither boring nor uncomfortable, however. This isn't the kind of stopped clock silence that occurs at 3:30 on a Friday afternoon when your work shift ends at 5:00. This is a gentle, musk-scented and blue-hued comfortable braking, and I believe it stems from using ASL. This language fosters a safe space; an opportunity, if you will, for my raggedy-faggedy, attention deficit disordered mind to cling to the present for more than one microsecond. Even in a location as audibly charged as a dance bar bear happy hour, talking with Sweet Sammy using ASL quiets things, makes them reasonable. The process of signing and reading signs directs my attention to what is real and present and in front of me, and removes the distracting pressure of cogitating on what I want to say in two minutes, or to that cute guy over there, or what I should have said when that bitch said that to me yesterday.

In reality, it's not time that slows down, it's me. And the ever-present and sense-obliterating noise doesn't fade; I just cease to pay attention to it. Engaging in this more intimate communication (ASL) narrows my intent, spotlights my focus, and this has improved my communication skills even though I am still basically a virgin at speaking the language.

Conversing in ASL forces direct communication. Although a rich language, ASL is also a series of shortcuts. Entire phrases and concepts that spoken languages take for granted are simply dropped off. Instead of saying "I think I'll go to the store for eggs and butter in just a few minutes", a deaf person would sign something approximating "I go store buy eggs butter". The elaborations – I think, in a few minutes, for, I will – are deemed unnecessary. Because of this, there are fewer opportunities for assumption and less of a tendency to "beat around the bush". No hemming and hawing in this language; deaf people tend to say exactly what they mean.

But more important to the art of communication, ASL fosters active listening by assuming that others will grant undivided attention to the speaker. My hearing friends and I don't give each other this gift. We continually talk over each other, ignore what each other says in order to cruise some hottie or begin a new conversation with a different friend, or interrupt each other if we have a point to make that we feel (we know!) is more important. This is not the case in ASL; the practicality of ASL requires that speakers take turns "at the podium" (signing) with only one person at a time holding court. The listeners are expected to watch the hands and the face of the person speaking – the hands because they form the words, the face because it portrays the emotion. The listeners politely hold their thoughts until the speaker has finished. Then and only then, at least in my limited experience, the listeners can retort. And only one at a time. Meanwhile, the original speaker listens just as intently and politely as others did while he spoke.

Because language and culture are so intimately entwined, this politeness extends beyond just conversation. Deaf culture feels more civilized in general than my other friendship groups. In the deaf world, it seems to me that everyone is afforded the opportunity to make their words known. It's an ultimately civilized mode of communication, and in this culture of civilized, polite, and direct communication, the exchange of ideas seems vastly improved.

Of course signing – and being the one hearing person in the midst of a group of deaf friends – isn't all roses and daffodils.

For starters, it's not an easy language to learn. The finger spelling alphabet is simple enough, but what right-minded person, deaf or hearing, who has an entire story to tell or thought to convey wants to spell every single word? Especially when there is an entire language available? None, that's who. But I am here to testify, Sister: this "entire language" isn't as easy to learn as might be imagined.

Not only is a new ASL speaker faced with learning syntax, grammar, and usage that are different from his spoken language(s), as anyone learning any new language is, he is also required to memorize a plethora of finger, hand, and arm movements, along with the attached facial expressions. Many of these signs and expressions have very subtle differences that, when used sloppily (as I've been accused of), convey a meaning nothing like what's intended. It can be downright embarrassing when you want to say something is your favorite and instead flip off an entire group of people. It's not unheard of. Ask several of my gay deaf friends who will recall the story with glee, I am sure.

Learning ASL can be difficult for the less-than-brilliant mind because it requires speakers to memorize and link a vast cognitive language structure to just as vast an array of tactile movements and expressions. It's a unique challenge.

As if that double-whammy language structure/physical component combination didn't throw me into a full-blown tailspin (I wonder how one signs that?), I've discovered that there is quite often contradictory colloquial use. Deaf people in, say, New York, sign things slightly differently than deaf people in, oh, Georgia. Or Tucson. And even among those located in one geographical area, one cohort can develop its own shortcuts and "dialect" which are independent of any other ASL education or pattern. The deaf guys at the bear happy hour have their own gay happy hour dialect, I am convinced. And finally, it seems deaf people have the option to use some variant along a continuum of ASL. This can range from pidgin (PSE), which is a blending of ASL, a distinct language, and English, to ASL, to SEE (Signing Exact English), a completely different language that follows exact English grammar and syntax. While each of these might contain similar elements, identical concepts or phrases are conveyed using entirely different movements and signs. It can be confusing even to deaf people. Imagine my bewilderment.

I offer a final observation from a bystander happily dipping his toes in this vibrant language and culture – notes from a newbie as it were. Sometimes being the one "hearie" in a group of ASL users can be isolating. One on one with a deaf person, the conversation goes pretty smoothly for me. The persons I have conversed with (especially if it is Sweet Sammy) quickly realize that I don't have a clue as to what I am really doing or saying, and each has been unwavering in patience and compassion. And willing to teach me as we go along.

However, get five or six deaf people together and that compassion flies out the window. Rightfully so –for them to not engage in their lively conversation would be akin to a group of English-speaking friends reverting to kindergarten level sentences in order to accommodate the one Spanish-speaking person in the group. The outsider (me) in these situations either keeps up or keeps quiet. But still I realize that the proverbial shoe is on the other foot and I have taken on the role of "disabled". Even at my beloved bear happy hour, in the midst of a group of deaf friends as I've watched fingers and faces fly at speeds I find unimaginable, it's been as though I'm hit by a mute brick dropped from ten floors above: here, I am the deaf one.

Funny, though; as my ASL skills increase, I am able to pick out enough individual signs to understand that the deaf gays also diss on the hottie or nottie over there, on which bitch has been back-stabbing which bitch, or on what improprieties have been occurring in their community. However, I do notice that even when being a bit ribald, it's done in their particularly polite manner.

When I am completely lost to the conversation, though, is when Sammy picks up the little notepad and carries on a nice side conversation with befuddled me. As I may have mentioned, he is nothing if not sweet.

BIRDS OF A FEATHER

A Two-Headed Bird

The Greyhound bus from New York lurches to a stop at the District of Columbia depot. Even before the door creaks open, cranky riders flock to the narrow aisle, pushing to be first off. They unfold legs stiff after four hours tucked at right angles behind tight seats. But Thomas Conrad remains seated. He sighs, and pats his short black afro into place with a well-manicured brown hand. He waits. Fourteen years in the US Air Force have instilled patience. And although this bus carries him homeward, home is not exactly where his heart rests. He does not hurry.

This man has two lives, but lives in neither. At the end of his work day, Lieutenant Colonel Conrad hangs the good soldier in the closet alongside the tidy service blues sporting medallions and decorations. The other half of this two-headed bird dons a different, but just as utilitarian, uniform. In sharp black shoes, shape-hugging jeans, and a crisp-pressed button-down shirt of four thin alternating vertical stripes – three in shades of sky blue and one of white - he dresses to impress. He readies for his personal life, his plumage carefully arranged with mating in mind.

But a problem arises as our preening Thomas navigates what are uncharted waters, for he has the distinction of being a man who seeks other men. His preference definitely flaps toward the softer side of the male spectrum – it is a feminine man he likes – but it is still men his interest flies toward. And despite the elimination of Don't Ask, Don't Tell, his preferences aren't something the Department of Defense embraces.

Or his African-American culture's church, for that matter.

"For God so loved the world that he gave his only begotten son, that whosoever believeth in him should not perish, but have everlasting life . . ." quoted the Reverend Hawken of the Almighty Bible Church of Tenlytown just last Sunday. His baritone commanded attention, and even though Thomas occupied his space in the family pew only out of a sense of familial duty, the message was still a source of chagrin.

Whosoever rings hollow in his experience with the good Reverend. *Whosoever* does not include *whatsoever*. And the punishment is a flight straight to hell. So Thomas hides his dates from family, from Uncle Sam, and from the church. Their gender never raises questions because no one ever meets them.

The cold truth illuminates, however: Thomas has *encounters*, not dates. Even after the repeal of Don't ask, Don't Tell, a real date poses a career-ending risk the duty-conscious soldier hasn't taken.

Still, a man has needs.

He seeks release in the shadows at the edge of life, flitting in dank recesses where secrecy thrives and men linger. Here he ventures unknown, unknowable. He moves undercover, incognito, and it comes easily; it's not a name the men crave.

But if they ask, he answers, "Call me Conrad."

"Oh, yeah, fuck, Conrad, that feels good. Yeah, man..."

They are secretive; they are not always quiet.

Of late, though, Thomas grows tired of these sideways glances at intimacy, but as much as he longs to look love straight in the eye, she is a bird that has remained hidden in the bush. In the void he settled for a temporary plunge in the wild side. His fever drew him to the crowded anonymity of the city to the north. New York beckoned with a throbbing member, and he answered the call. He flew the coop.

Over the New Year's holiday weekend, for four sleepless days and nights, he was unfettered Thomas. Queer Thomas. Drunken Thomas. Loosey-goosey Thomas grooving on the dance floor. Thomas escorting the smooth young chicken to his room.

"Oh, man," they mumbled, tumbling behind the locked doors. "Mmmmm, good."

But now he returns. He steps from the bus and makes his way through the worn bus depot toward the taxi queue outside. As he exits the building, his bag trailing like a tired duckling, the frigid winter air slaps him full in the face with an icy palm.

"Party's over," it says. "Welcome home."

Thomas nestles deeper into the collar of his leather faux-motorcycle jacket as he walks to the first cab waiting at the curb.

"18th and R," he instructs the driver as he settles in the back seat.

A Bird of a Different Color

T'Shayda Johnson is, well, pink. There's no other way to describe her. She's a long-legged, fresh-faced, red-dreaded flamingo of a woman. Kind of, anyway. T'Shayda isn't really a chick at all, you see. Not biological. Not that you would know right off the bat. Her size might be a clue; she's almost six feet tall. But T'Shayda has the swish in her walk and the sashay in her talk. Once you get past the size, T'Shayda's womanhood is without question.

And that drove her mother as crazy as a loon.

"Todd Shane Johnson, get your butt back in here and take off that make-up, take off that dress, get rid of those earrings and undo that hair. You are not leaving this house like that," T'Shayda's mother admonished all through the teen years. She sure didn't understand who had fledged from her loins; she didn't want to understand. And the church was no help. At least to T'Shayda.

God, in the voice of the same Reverend Hawken, somber in black silk robes over a custom-tailored businessman's suit, from his pulpit on high at the Almighty Bible Church of Tenlytown, just after he asked for tithing, instructed T'Shayda's mother to toss her to the streets. This was eight years ago, when T'Shayda was a tender seventeen.

"When it comes to our attention that a member of our flock strays from the teachings of the Bible, when one of our fold admits that homosexuality tempts, when he or she embraces those teachings of Satan, we have no choice. We must throw them out," the good Reverend had preached that grey October Sunday.

T'Shayda's mother took the words to heart. If this philosophy is righteous enough for the voice of her God, then it works for her. The rotten egg has got to go. No more wringing of her hands; she washed them of this abomination. T'Shayda was tossed out.

But T'Shayda is nothing if not resourceful, and a statuesque gender-bender can make a living if she applies herself properly. T'Shayda applied herself three or four times a day at first, just to survive. But as her clientele grew and her rates increased, she was able to apply herself less frequently. At the age of twenty-five, T'Shayda has applied herself to management. No bird brain here, she has a head for the business. Now she runs a house for nestlings just like her: boy-girls cast out by families who don't understand, all come to find a loving home and tidy income under T'Shayda's careful watch. These little birds have not only endured the pain of being tossed from the aerie, they have learned to soar.

T'Shayda says a God far more just than the Reverend Hawken's provided this life for her. Her girls agree.

But right now T'Shayda's brood needs fed, and since Mother's cupboards are bare, she finds herself flying to the market. She throws a pink fur-lined jacket over her emerald green velour jogging suit, wraps a purple paisley scarf over her head, and traipses through the ice and snow in her fuzzy bedroom slippers to the corner. In short order a cab pulls over.

Birds on the Wing

An unfamiliar landscape whizzes by as the cab traverses the city. Thomas' vernacular ends with the imposing Pentagon military complex just across the Potomac River and the turn-of-the-century mansions of the DuPont neighborhood, with their seedy corners and cock-hungry men. He knows no middle ground.

When the cab abruptly pulls over at an anonymous corner, Thomas is momentarily alarmed, but his ruffled feathers soon settle. Capitalism operates vis-à-vis supply-and-demand, which extends through the food chain to the cabbies. The driver spots a potential second fare: two birds with one stone. No cause for alarm.

"Where are you going?" the driver squawks through the opened window.

"Giant," chirps the tall woman on the corner.

Amazon, Thomas thinks. But beautiful.

"Get in," says the cabbie.

She alights behind the driver and turns to survey Thomas, who roosts at the opposite end of the back seat. The purple paisley scarf she wears over her head falls casually to her shoulders, followed by her long red dreadlocks. She extends a hand. French manicure, he notes. Big hands.

"I'm T'Shayda," she warbles. She twinkles. Her voice plays and her eyelashes flutter seductively.

"Hello, I'm Thomas" he answers, addressing the flapping eyelashes. They hold his attention.

"Are you from out of town?" T'Shayda asks. The vigor of the eyelash fluttering increases. Her professional life has been good, lucrative, but she, too, longs for something more intimate. She has been around this block enough times to recognize the well-dressed man next to her as one of the flock, and she is attracted to his quiet, stalwart substance. The mating song begins.

"Nope," Thomas replies.

"Oh, I see." T'Shayda pays no mind to his brevity. "I see you are a traveler, so you're coming home, then?'

"Yep."

"From where?"

"New York," Thomas replies. He didn't feel like chatting but this girl's freshness has encouraged him. She's unusual. Something about her demeanor says that she has battled adversity face-to-face, yet her confident air implies that she crowed victory. She glows with open and unafraid playfulness. Engaging. If only she were a man, Thomas muses, sarcastically.

T'Shayda coos, "I love New York! Were you there for New Year's? What part of the city? What hotel? I love staying in fancy hotels. I adore it. I have room service. And the spa. Of course some old rooster pays for it, but that's OK; it's my business and my business is good."

Thomas contemplates this dove's matter-of-fact revelation without fear or harsh judgment. He applauds her honesty and admires her strength. He can be no more judgmental of her than she is of herself. Her trilling song mesmerizes him; her beauty captivates. He listens. He watches. Her pinked lips pout artistically; her egg cream skin illuminates from within. Her fine features taper to a long, elegant neck. Her Adam's apple bobs as she chats.

Adam's apple?

This charming goose is a gander in disguise.

Thomas sparks; a kinship fires. They are a pink-hued flamingo standing elegantly against an azure tropical sky and a slick-bodied, ice-bound, uniform-clad penguin, but they are both avian.

Thomas imagines himself perched on a high wire. A four-star General waves a medal of good conduct from the safe-haven at one end while this unique creature flashes her come-hither smile at the other. Both are just out of reach, and he fears moving in either direction. He will fall. Thomas balances precariously and dangerously in the middle, frozen, flightless.

"Hello?" T'Shayda interrupts his fantasy.

"The Village. I stayed in the Village." Thomas snaps back, too quickly. But T'Shayda doesn't notice. Her warbling continues.

"Oh, honey, the village. You hear that, driver? I love the village. That's my part of town," T'Shayda pipes. She places one bejeweled hand on the driver's shoulder, gently, as though she were coddling an egg. "You might need to go to the village, sir. Do you some good. You could get some. When's the last time you had some?"

The driver laughs and waves T'Shayda away. He has seen much more than a cross-dressing prostitute in his cab. This beauty is anything but frightening to him.

"My people hang out in the Village," T'Shayda says to both of them. "We feel safe there. Birds of a feather, you know . . . and people don't judge a book by its cover in the Village."

"I'm guessing I'm your people, then," Thomas admits, and then continues, "and you . . . your cover . . . ?" He hesitates, unsure of how to ask.

"I live in my own skin," T'Shayda replies, simply.

"Do you . . . uhm . . . is it . . .? His stuttering persists.

She laughs, and without drawing the attention of the driver, she uses a manicured fist to heft the bulge tucked in the nest of her velour pants.

"I see," Thomas notes, and continues, "Does it . . .?" He arches his eyebrows upward, wing-like, to finish the question.

She responds without pause, looking directly into his eyes, "Like a geyser." And then, immediately, "I hate grocery shopping. Look at this. I am out here on Sunday afternoon in my house slippers. Lordy, house slippers! Like some kind of barnyard biddy. Do you need a wife, sir?" she asks the driver without skipping a beat. "I can be your wife. I can pass."

"No, no," laughs the driver, his eyes twinkling with good humor as they make contact with Thomas' in the mirror. "I have a wife, 32 years. I don't need another wife."

"I'll treat you right," she says flirtatiously. The driver giggles. T'Shayda's playfulness is contagious. It rubs off.

She turns to face Thomas again. "You're nice to let him pick me up. I would have told him to keep moving. Don't pick up that thing. I'm tired. I would have said, 'Keep drivin', sir.' He's just trying to get more money, you know."

The driver merely shrugs while Thomas and T'Shayda share a laugh. She does pass, Thomas realizes.

"I could never say that," he ventures. "You are much too pretty to leave out in the snow."

T'Shayda pulls the scarf from her shoulders and drapes it over Thomas' broad frame.

"You're pretty now, too," she says with a warm smile.

They all laugh again, and they are still laughing as the taxi makes a turn into the parking lot of the Giant Food Store. As it waits for a chain-dangling, tattooed Latino teen who struts without worry or haste across the drive, T'Shayda resumes the conversation.

"Air Force?" she asks.

"Uhm," Thomas stammers. He flushes with embarrassment; it seems he can only stammer in her presence. "How do you know?"

"Honey," she replies, leaning toward him and letting one hand fall to rest on his knee, "T'Shayda has been through it. I've seen plenty in my life. I've been tossed to the curb and I've picked myself right back up. And I've seen that frozen look in many a soldier's face. You are expected to give your life, but you don't get one in return. Makes me furious."

Thomas returns to the high wire of his imagination, but this time as he looks down from his tenuous perch, he sees the paisley scarf stretched below, a silken purple safety net. He tiptoes along the quivering strand toward T'Shayda.

"You could just tell?" he wonders aloud.

She laughs. "Christ no. You dropped your military I.D. It's there on the floor."

Indeed. Thomas peers between his feet and sees his own face peering back. He retrieves the I.D., sheepishly.

"You must feel like the ugly duckling, the odd man out. I've known the feeling. But let me assure you, you're a swan. And you can trust T'Shayda. T'Shayda asks, but T'Shayda don't tell. And I would like to know you better, and I don't mean business. Remember this if nothing else: 202-379-5453. It's easy. Repeat after me: 202-379-5453."

"202-379-5453," he repeats, parrot-like. He will not forget.

She winks. He smiles. She smiles. He thaws. On the high wire, he stretches out a hand and she catches it with hers. She pulls him close; they fly away.

The cab pulls up to the door of the Giant Food Market and T'Shayda pays the driver. She gives Thomas a quick peck on the cheek before she steps out.

"Happy New Year, lover" T'Shayda shoots back through the open door. And then she closes it. She blows Thomas another kiss before turning to walk through the store's entrance, pink slippers slapping against the cold concrete. Thomas continues thawing as the cab pulls back into traffic.

And then they drive in silence, Thomas still wearing the scarf.

The Flocking Instinct

"Nice neighborhood. You have restaurants, nightlife. It's all close. And you don't have to worry about crime here," the driver says as he pulls the cab to the side at 18th and R.

Thomas doesn't tell him about being mugged on this very corner. He lost the seventeen dollars he had in his pocket and the cheap watch from his wrist. The hooded thug said he had a gun, and Thomas hadn't argued. The thief's eyes were brimming with desperation, and that was all he needed to know. Thomas had done exactly as he was told.

But that seems far away to him. Another lifetime. If it happened today, he might just fly over the thief's head.

"Seven dollars," the driver says.

Thomas hands him a twenty-dollar bill. "Eight back is fine."

"Thank you, sir, thank you. Happy New Year," the driver gushes.

"Yes," Thomas crows to the neighborhood as he steps to the curb. "Happy New Year."

As he gathers his bag and surveys his waiting home, Thomas slides the silky fabric of T'Shayda's paisley scarf through his fingers. He presses it to his face and inhales. He will wear it until he returns it, and it will remind him of life's possibilities until T'Shayda can remind him in person.

Thomas fishes in his pocket for his keys as he looks up to the gathering haze of the winter twilight. A single raven flies overhead, cawing, cawing, as though searching for something. From somewhere distant, unseen, another raven answers. The lone raven turns in mid-air and flies toward the answer in the dusk.

SWIMMING UPSTREAM, JUNE CLEAVER ON MY MIND

That summer morning during my eighteenth year, 1976, I dove into the unknown. Until then I had floated in the unusual but predictable pool of my rural Wyoming, large-family childhood. As one of the younger of seven boys born to an overburdened farmwife and an absent, mean-spirited father, I grew up feral. Despite my family's chronic TV habit, we were definitely not the Cleavers.

I doggie-paddled through unintentional parental neglect and belly flopped into high school high-jinx. I was a member of the largest class to date to graduate from Riverside High School (32 students), and we were reckless. True to the times, our focus was sex, drugs, rock and roll.

My high school sweetheart was an older married woman. It was an unconventional coming-of-age story, but given my marijuana-inspired-free-love peers, somehow normal. When her angry bear of a husband found out, though, it ended. Not-so-gentle Ben hissed my marching orders and punctuated them with the sharp point of a hunting knife. Like a deer in the headlights, I was as petrified as topiary but at the last second bounded into the underbrush. I narrowly escaped the thud of impact.

I packed my Fleetwood Mac cassette tapes and Levi's button-fly jeans, said my good-byes, and turned away from my miscreant youth. I pointed my gargantuan Chrysler Newport south and punched the gas. I was free. I may have been pushed into the flow, but I swam with joy.

I got as far as Salt Lake City before the gravity of my poverty yanked me to a standstill. Twilight: the gas gauge needle rested on the big red E as I pulled over on the first rise of hills above the city. The lights below were oceanic, twinkling fluid yet substantial. Come morning I sold the Newport and began searching for meaning.

I was swept away at first, unmoored in the currents of a world moving faster than anticipated. I was able to land an acceptable job considering that I had no education or skills; I trolled with bare hooks and luck provided the basics for me. But a sense of belonging proved to be more elusive. It taunted me from the murky depths of my desire then scurried away from my groping fingers. I dated but no bond formed. The path to coupledom seemed blocked by a solid piece of me planted firmly in the way. I could find no route around myself, no ladder to a higher me. After the exhilaration of backstroking away from my delinquency, I floated in a sinkhole. I feared I would drown.

But I didn't.

Instead, I found a therapist. He administered tests – hundreds of seemingly meaningless statements I was asked to agree or disagree with. *I look at my stool after I defecate. I sometimes cross the street to avoid talking to someone I know. I have thoughts of killing myself.*

I could decipher no code, no right or wrong, so I answered truthfully. Later the therapist called me to his office and looked at me with intelligent brown eyes that brimmed with understanding.

"You are gay," He said, placing one comforting hand on my knee, and it's OK to be gay. Enjoy your life."

I dove again, this time into the depths of my generation's rebellion. We marched. *We're here, we're queer, get used to it.* And we played. It was a glittering free-style underworld of disco balls, highballs, and swingin' balls.

I wish I could remember more of 1978. In photos I am rail-thin in platform shoes and bell-bottom plaid trousers. I sport floppy curls, a mischievous smile, and glassy eyes. I had fun, but only two years after my back flip into the deep end of "enjoying my life", I had over-punched my dance card.

Over-punched is understated; it was tattered.

I had done more drugs than some twice my age, all washed down with vodka. Followed by men. But the buzzed nights of music and trysts became cliché. What had been a glorious subsurface romp with like-minded lads grew dull. We were junior barracudas feeding on good times and each other like there was no tomorrow, but I always knew that tomorrow would come. This flashing impermanence frightened me. June Cleaver would not have approved.

I saw the therapist again. "Is it OK to love someone?" I asked.

"Yes. Me," he eventually answered.

Living as an open same-sex couple in Salt Lake City *in front of God and everybody* was somehow more taboo than marching down State Street or playing nasty in the dark recesses of gay bars, which made it an essential act for those who lived to push the limits. We bought a condo, furniture, china, and stemware. We wanted a puppy but the condo association refused. We got goldfish instead; they died with alarming frequency.

With some experience and the beginnings of a secondary education, I was no longer the smallest fish in the pond. I already earned more money than my parents ever had, and I spent more than they could imagine. I shopped my way through disagreements and pretended I was blissfully happy, just like those damn Cleavers. I circled my bowl like the current goldfish until I, too, felt like I could die from the sheer boredom of it.

It ended like a flash flood. A small argument boiled over, my emotions exploded, and I marched back into the stream of life to continue my quest to belong. I jerked through the remainder of my twenties and the first years of my thirties, always looking, never finding. I called four different cities home, had six different jobs, eight different boyfriends. My life was segmented and each stopover was like a dip in a deck pool, but as soon as the water became comfortable I flopped across the splintery deckboards and hurtled myself over the edge. I was a salmon escaping the net; I returned to the cold water to navigate closer to *belonging*. I lurched toward the next iteration of me.

I was a cowboy driving a truck in Denver, a grunge boy on a bike in Seattle. I picked up a southern accent and a Puerto Rican in

Charlotte, I learned to eat crawdads. I taught aerobics in DC, I quit smoking.

I searched through my thirties, swimming up the wrong fork in the stream on more than one occasion. Although my mistakes sometimes devolved into frantic back-paddling, it was never without merit. I took my lessons as they came.

I wandered into the wrong bar at the right time, met a man who showed interest in me when my self-interest was flailing. I hovered near the buoy of this married man for five years and learned how to share a partner, a skill that has served me well since.

I cannon-balled into a bathhouse and met another. We moved east and this time we got the dog. She stayed with him when he realized I wasn't true. I navigated back across the county in a pale yellow Yugo. Just west of Oklahoma I encountered a blizzard and arrived "home" in Colorado minutes before I-70 was closed. I counted my blessings.

I floated with serendipity, open to what came. A friend happened to mention that the owners of his apartment building were looking for a new manager. I lived rent free and learned to sell. *There's a seat for every ass*, I discovered. I tired of commuting to a belligerent boss and applied for a job I wasn't qualified for. I may have fluffed my resume, but by week three in the position I had learned what I needed. I faked my way to proficiency. I listened to the voices around me and picked up the cues I needed. I prepared, dove, assimilated. I would have been a good alien invader.

I was attracted to artists. I loved the dancer's body below me; I twisted him into positions no other could attain. I was captivated by the angry thrust of the stage director. I caught then released the actor; the flip-flops from comedy to drama were too unpredictable for even me. I appreciated the steadiness of the textile artist but he soon became as one-dimensional as his medium. The opera's wigmaker was my wild child. He introduced me to Puccini and HIV. They both seemed inevitable.

Experience deepened me; I drew closer to myself. I gave up artists when I began to seriously write. I had discovered my own creative flow.

At forty-three, real love caught up with me for the first time. He was a soldier and spoke so quietly that I was forced to listen. I stopped thrashing and his sweet voice filled my head with dreams. In crisp blues and with a plain face, he asked for my company. He didn't demand, and he didn't hesitate. He stood stalwart and accepted me: my past, my present, what I might become in the future. I dove into his stream. No choice. No regret. Love was ours to make.

Ten years passed and each day dawned new, each morning was another party in a private pool for two. Holding hands we moved upstream together. One lead while one rested, pulled along in the drag of the other. We dealt with dying parents, our own ever more infirm bodies, and the on-going chaos of the world. We certainly weren't the Cleavers, but we thrived. Swimming in pairs, I learned, is my calling. It is how I belong.

A FISTFUL OF SERENITY

Blood was bound to be shed, that was a given. Only question was – whose? Perhaps the woman behind him in the ticket line – maybe then her yammering would stop.

"Dang, one clerk," she groused. She was tall and thin, pole-like, somewhat unkempt. And she twitched. Nervously. "Doggone, it's only the first day of the Clint Eastwood retrospective. They didn't know there'd be a line?"

But Bobby ignored her. He agreed it was asinine that only one teenaged cashier handled the queue, but he was in no mood to chat. Especially with this canary-in-a-coal-mine. He tuned out her twittering, studied the digital orange letters on the marquee instead. Not that he had to. He had chosen this theater because he needed an Eastwood blood bath, and any one of them would do. He just wanted to watch Clint prove, as he always did, that what's right wasn't always pretty or easy. But it was always necessary.

Fidgeting Woman pressed closer behind him. Her long chin nearly hooked over his right shoulder and her moist breath trickled down the back of his neck.

"This line is barely moving. I'm never going to get a good seat. I hate sitting too close. Or too far away." She spat her worry at him, but her voice softened as she continued, "Clint Eastwood is such a man's man. All the ladies love him. You know he has seven kids? He was sixty-six years old when the last one was born. They have five different mothers. Plus he's been with lots of other women. Barbra Streisand, for one."

Some other day Bobby might not have reacted so harshly to her rapid-fire outpouring of trivia. After all, he agreed with her. Eastwood *was* the man. A real stud. And any guy who had been with Streisand deserved idolatry. But today this woman's anxiety was too real, too palpable, too close. He had to get away from her. Bobby stepped aside, barely out of the ticket line, and turned an insular back. He focused on the movie times with fresh intensity.

"What are you looking at? Did they change the times? Is it sold out?" She moved to his side and studied the marquee with him. She raveled and unraveled a disintegrating white tissue with a quick, jerking motion and then ran her fingers through the slack hair framing her face.

Bobby wished he was here with his mother – catching movies from "the old-days" was one of the special things they shared. She was gracefully enamored of *The Man With No Name*, unlike this blathering

Fidgeting Woman. If Mom was here she'd wink at him and whisper, "God grant me the serenity to accept the things I cannot change . . ."

But today he was alone, and instead of hearing his mother's sweet prayer, he heard Fidgeting Woman. Her nasal whine bludgeoned his every nerve.

"Hey! No cuts!"

Without him or Fidgeting Woman noticing, someone had taken *their* spot in line.

"*Go ahead, make my day,*" Bobby said.

When he visited his mother earlier, he let himself in with the skeleton key he'd had since childhood. His mother used to make him wear it on a string around his neck; she was afraid he would lose it. But now it dangled from his key ring alongside the new-fangled electronic fob that unlocked his waterfront condo, and the thick key to his busy theater costume studio.

The family brownstone usually provided a cool respite from the brutal heat and humidity of the Washington, DC August afternoons, the thick brocade drapes he and his mother stitched years ago on her old Singer machine drawn tight in defense. But today the house had felt worn and stale, and had been permeated with the awful scent that had been there since the cancer took hold of his mother.

"Mom? Hello? Mom!" he had called out. There was no answer. He climbed the stairs and walked the long, dim upper hallway. All the while he feared what he might find. She might be spilled over the stairs in a cascade of death. Or permanently at rest in one of the old wingchairs in the upper landing. Or worse. She could be puddled on the bathroom floor. He would find her heaped on the tiny hexagonal tiles, her thin cotton robe wrenched up over the leaking blue adult diaper in a final act of dehumanization. The ugly end.

But when he looked through the partially open door of her boudoir he saw that she was still flat on her back on the hospital bed. Her wrists intersected over her chest, corpse-like, and her feet, the one part of her that hadn't shriveled, were splayed. Highlighted in bright white orthopedic hose, they dwarfed her deflated body.

Bobby stared across the dim distance of her bedroom, but there was no sign of life. No twitch, no spasm, no movement at all. He turned an ear to better hear, but there was no sound, either. Not a snore, a wheeze, or a rattle. Nothing.

He moved to her bedside, holding his breath against that sickening odor, and looked down at her, at the dry flakes of her scalp beneath the thin fuzz of white hair and the way her lower jaw hung open. *If she's passed*, he thought, *I should close her mouth before rigor mortis locks it open. She would hate anyone seeing her like this.*

Bobby trembled as he lifted one hand from the crossbones over her heart. His third grade teacher had used a pair of caged rabbits to teach the class the miracle of reproduction, perhaps to sway back to the heterosexual fold those she suspected were already moving away from that calling. His mother's hand felt very much like the wriggling pink newborn Miss Knapp had pressed hopefully into his small palm. Hairless skin sliding over the lumps and bulges of delicate bones. A clawing infant mammal, his mother's gnarled claw. Panic.

Then her fingers fluttered in his and she awoke. They both exhaled as her rheumy eyes focused. "Bobby," she whispered.

He moved her dead weight to the bedside wheelchair and gave her two of the Oxycodone that no longer kept her pain at bay. Then he retreated toward the kitchen to heat some soup for her lunch, detouring to the back porch for fresh air and a cigarette. The nicotine settled his nerves. A lawnmower buzzed in the distance and the sound of boys at play dribbled over the fences separating the back lots along the alley. Bobby remembered his own solitary childhood, the hours spent in the sewing room with his mother, the other boys' taunts as he hurried home from school.

"Hey, *Roberta*, going in to help your mama sew now?"

He had kept current with these boys' lives through the years. Even after moving across town, he came home every day for lunch. His mother fed him the neighborhood news along with whatever she had cooked. Vincent was sent to jail, she told him over meatloaf. Tax fraud. Edward lost his job and their family's home. Tyrone was in rehab. Again.

Bobby butted the cigarette in the powdery dirt beneath some potted marigolds gone dead from neglect. It was time to heat the soup.

These days she barely woke when he brought her the lunch he fixed. She just sat with her chin resting on the bones of her chest, her involuntarily gaping mouth forced shut by the weight of her head. But today, when Bobby hooked the tray over the arms of the wheelchair, she stirred and shifted in the green plastic seat. She lifted the spoon and then, as she did before every meal, she recited her favorite prayer. "God grant me the serenity to accept the things I cannot change, the courage to change the things I can, and the wisdom to know the difference."

The words elicited a familiar memory, but this time it spilled across him hard like an avalanche. The vignette was unremarkable, but he remembered every detail. Twilight sliced horizontally across the room. She was a young woman; Bobby was still a toddler. She leaned over the white enameled side rail of his crib and recited the prayer in a sing-song voice. Her dark hair was pleated into a thick braid that tumbled over one shoulder. She smelled like Lux soap, and the wallpaper behind her was – still was today – pale ivory and festooned with clumps of dark purple plums and bright green, teardrop-shaped leaves. When she left the nursery, a wicker laundry basket perched on one hip, she paused in the doorway and smiled back at him. And then he was alone with the fruits and her words. First memory.

Twenty-seven words he had heard for forty-seven years. Diaper rash, father's burial, puberty's angst, his sexuality – all scabs his mother soothed with the salve of this prayer. Over time the words inserted themselves in his reflexes. At first blush of pain or bruise of ego, his mother's calm voice came to him: accept or change, but do so wisely.

Today, though, she barely eked out the words, more a plea than a prayer, and then without swallowing even one bite of soup she dropped the spoon and asked to be put back to bed.

"Bobby, this is no way to live," she mumbled before closing her eyes.

"It's going to be OK," he answered as he smoothed her fly-away hair, "I promised." But she didn't hear him. Her mouth fell open as she drifted off.

The scent of greasy popcorn curled Bobby's stomach as Line Cutter gave him and Fidgeting Woman the evil eye. "You two better not fuck with me. I didn't cut; you were looking at the marquee. I just got in line while you were making up your minds."

Fidgeting Woman huffed. "I was in line. I already know what I am seeing. *A Fistful of Dollars*. You cut."

Bobby just laughed. "Look," he said, pointing to Fidgeting Woman. "*The Good . . .*" He pointed to himself. "*The Bad . . .*" and then he pointed to Line Cutter. "*And the Ugly.*"

Just then the line moved forward and, like a steam engine crossing the vast landscape in one of the old spaghetti westerns, they all chugged closer to Clint. Bobby and the woman moved back into line but the squatter held fast and hobbled forward with them. When they stalled again, he and Bobby stood face-to-face. From beneath the mop of his tousled black hair, Line Cutter's needle-sharp eyes stabbed at Bobby.

"You looking for a fight, faggot?" Line Cutter punctuated his question with a sharp poke to the chest, a one-fingered shove that caught Bobby off guard. He stumbled backwards.

Bobby's mother always arched her brows during the second line of the supplication. They angled up toward God, stretched up like hands rising in a hallelujah chorus. Those eyebrows had faith in the message. ". . . the courage to change the things I can," she would say, forehead clasped in prayer.

After pouring the soup down the disposal and rinsing the dishes, Bobby had wandered the quiet house. Every nook held a secret;

every window jamb and cabinet pull prompted a memory. Here was where his mother found his father laid out after the heart attack. Everyone had always said it would be the drink that got him, but he fooled them.

That credenza held his mother's purse, middle drawer on the right. Bobby had pilfered smokes from it, hiding and choking in the garage until it felt natural. In later years he and his mother would share cigarettes like they shared their best-friend secrets.

And that is the table at which his mother served the soup *she* warmed for *him*.

Everything in the brownstone was familiar yet unfamiliar, all of it an askew rendition of what used to be. The rooms seemed smaller than they once were, and as Bobby paced their limits the walls heaved further inward. And that horrid, acidic scent persevered. He repeated his mother's prayer over and over.

At the foot of the stairs, a loose floorboard squeaked beneath the outdated orange and yellow carpet. It used to be he knew every loose board, every noise the old floor made. In his teens, he crept through the nighttime shadows of this house, slunk out undetected to meet like-minded boys and returned, hours later, beneath his mother's loving radar. But there was no longer reason to sneak. Even if she hadn't years ago embraced the life her only son lived, what remained upstairs was no longer her.

Bobby rocked back and forth on the disjointed plank, his left hand caressing the smooth round finial at the banister's end. The floorboard protested with a steady rhythm – squeak-squeak, squeak-

squeak, squeak-squeak – like a persistent, nagging heartbeat. He slowed his movement until the sound ceased. Dead silence.

Bobby made his way back to his mother's side. There, he hovered.

Her chest lifted and fell in a shallow but regular pattern, her heart and lungs refusing to stop even though the rest of her body had given up. Again her mouth dangled open. The toothless pink cavern glistened in the dim light.

Bobby lifted the spare pillow, fluffed its feathers, and then pressed it to her face. He pushed hard, a hand on each side of the head to seal the mouth and nose. The body convulsed once, twice, and then the right arm weakly flailed. It made one reflexive, aimless punch that connected with nothing, and then settled gently back to the bed. All was still. Bobby kept pressing on the pillow, and between his sobs he counted aloud in a slow-paced rhythm: "One, two, three . . .," all the way to twenty. He had to make certain the deed was done; there was no turning back. When he finally removed the pillow she didn't move. He wiped his eyes and felt for a pulse on her wrist and then her neck. Nothing.

Bobby closed his mother's mouth but it fell open again, so he lifted the surprising heft of her head and wadded the guilty pillow beneath it. Her face tipped forward; her mouth latched shut. And that is how he left her for Miss Agnes, the visiting nurse, to find.

Line Cutter swung wide. His powerful arm ended in a tight fist that connected with the left side of Bobby's head, knocking him to the garish carpet. Fidgeting Woman scurried to the cashier without a backwards glance as Line Cutter hurled himself at Bobby, throwing wild punches that crunched into his face. But Bobby felt no pain. He felt only the blood pouring from his nose. It was warm, red absolution. Then two policemen yanked the slugger off him and it was over.

He mouthed *thank you* to Line Cutter as he was dragged away.

Bobby retreated to the men's room to wash. Calmed, bleeding stopped, he returned to the now-empty queue. He paid for a ticket and begged a cup of ice, and then made his way toward the dark, safe embrace of the theater. The previews had begun, and in the faint blue light of the projector Bobby saw Fidgeting Woman squirming in her seat. He moved as far away as possible, where he held the ice to the swelling tenderness of his face and waited for the movie to begin.

"And the wisdom to know the difference," Bobby said to no one in particular.

WHILE WAITING
FOR MY BELOVED'S ARRIVAL
AT SACRAMENTO INT'L AIRPORT

A chubby, chubby girl wearing too-tight Apple Bottom jeans waits for someone's flight - delayed - while surreptitiously devouring a Cinnabon. "It's not my fault; I am forced to linger," her furtive expression implies as she wipes all evidential traces of icing from her chin. To her right, an antique couple decomposed by time – nothing left but decrepitude and mildew-tinged aroma – fuss with tickets, passports, carry-ons, and directions, effectively blocking the only 'up' escalator for latecomers rushing to their gates. "C Terminal, Grandma," someone yells in passing. "Go that way!"

A soldier in wrinkled camouflage gear returns from the unwarranted war. The shell-shocked, culture-shocked, blank-eyed stranger-in-his-own-town is greeted by no one. He stands apart, watching for his duffel to tumble down the conveyor. Private Lonely smoothes the ruffled fringes of his scalp with his fingers; he is overdue for a trim. A business traveler strides by, too close, oblivious, his expensive heels tapping on the beige tile floor. His premium dress suggests financial prowess. With a Bluetooth attached to his left ear, he is "trying to wrap my head around the business plan, Joe."

A clan of foreigners, their flamboyant attire and rapid gibberish met with great disdain by less remarkable travelers, reply with long, defiant stares, sensing their relative safety in numbers. Their children play on the uncomfortable plastic seating like any children. Across the barren expanse of the waiting area a different child rejoices. Her mother appears; an unexpected early arrival. If only I was as fortunate. "Mama! Mama! Mama!" the girl screeches. It is an earsplitting notification that, unlike me, all is once again whole in her world.

A woman weeps at her twin's departure, the voice of reason and empathy in this, her world of treason. The sister leaves and she is alone again with that man who pulls her roughly, crying, toward the exit. Another man gently maneuvers his companion to a corner for a semi-private good-bye. He places his hand on the small of her back and presses toward her; mouth pursed and tongue at the ready. She stiffens, leans away, and pecks him once on the cheek. He tries again; she pats his chest and averts her lips anew. Her eyes don't stray from the Arrival/Departure board.

Hurry now, my beloved, your flight is late and I wait at this crossroads where shards of the human race gather. Some arrive, the lucky shove off, and the rest of us sit, marooned. By coincidence alone we fragments share this time and space. We are misaligned pieces from different jigsaw puzzles and none of our edges snap together, yet somehow we still connect to produce an image most complete. But hurry now, I wait.

CHERRY: THE FAT MAN'S STORY

Night falls. A dark velvet curtain settles over the ground-hugging, drab features of the dusty township located far from the city life with its high-rise lofts and fashion shows, its martini happy hours and gay ghetto. Night falls here far, far away from the life most of us know. But night falls on this life, regardless.

A stone's-throw from the edge of the village, squatting as if to seek refuge from the impending darkness, amid ancient and twisted cottonwood trees, sits a house. In truth, not so much a house as a collection of huts, each built for some other purpose and moved here from some distant location to be joined together in haphazard and thoughtless fashion, bound at the seams with found nails and salvaged wood. The house grew over the years by bits and pieces, rooms added to the central space, growing outward like crippled spider's legs, each appendage tacked on to accommodate the next bastard son's arrival.

The small living room, the center of this web of weatherworn wood and dirty windows that for the most part reveal nothing more than the wall of the addition next-door, changes as the day ends. One grimy pane opens to a thin slice of the murky sky, admitting enough receding sunlight to cast faint shadows that steadily lengthen, and then join together in an increasing depth of gray until they are no longer separate, and finally disappear altogether in the darkness. Night falls, heavily.

On a tattered and food-stained La-Z-Boy recliner, in a shapeless afghan bathrobe – once a bright pink and turquoise flower print but now worn to a threadbare, nondescript non-color – sprawls a very large man. It is not important that we know his name. For our purposes, he is known simply as the Fat Man.

The Fat Man blends into the settling darkness, the outline of his ample features blurring until the only indication of his presence is the sporadic movement of his fleshy hand from the box of chocolate-covered cherries to his mouth and back again, his arm repeating the pattern like an intermittent and slow piston that powers the continuous and faster motion of the grinding-chewing-mashing of the chocolates in his mouth. In the silence of the sullen night the only sounds are the 'whoosh' of his fleshy underarm against the side of his even fleshier breast and the 'click-clack-pop' of his dentures as he chews. Whoosh-click-clack-pop. Click-clack-pop. Click-clack-pop. Muffled and repetitive, like the gloom that surrounds him. In this darkness, in the center of the web of this house of pain, with no comfort and no companion, he eats.

The candies are pedestrian, more paraffin than chocolate but more refined sugar than anything else. He purchased five boxes at the Script-All Pharmacy at half price because the expiration date had passed. The other four boxes have been consumed over the past four nights.

"Self-control," he tells himself, mumbling aloud as he hunkers in the hunkered house in the dark, in this collection of shacks that so concisely mirrors his haphazard family, "is eating only one box each night." He tells himself this even though only one box does very little to ease the vague, empty ache he attributes to his stomach, without ever suspecting the truth of its origin: his soul.

He takes one candy from the box and holds it in his warm hand. The chocolate paraffin begins to melt. He plays a waiting game with these chocolates. He plays a game with most food. He waits a full three minutes between candies, but not a moment longer. Without benefit of a watch, by instinct alone, he gently holds each chocolate in his hand for exactly three minutes. He has played this game for years, long enough to know, without counting, the very second those three minutes end.

"Practice", he has repeated and repeated and repeated to himself, "makes perfect."

Through practice he has made perfect the counting of three minutes. In three minutes, exactly three minutes, the chocolate is perfect – soft, ripe, ready. In his perfect world, practice makes perfect the counting off of the time required to make perfect chocolate. It is his perfect world.

The chocolate softens. His life remains the same. The dull ache in his stomach deepens. Three minutes pass; he has met his goal. The piston rotates, the chocolate is deposited in his mouth, and the chewing begins: whoosh-click-clack-pop. Click-clack-pop. Click-clack-pop.

The perfectly softened chocolate has left a smear in his palm, and he raises his hand toward the weak light of the moon through the grease-smeared glass. His eyes trace the pattern of the dark chocolate against his puffy white skin, and he reads it like a gypsy reads tealeaves. Vignettes of his uninspired life play in his mind. In the darkness, with the melted candy on his fat-swollen palm, he thinks of the little bastards. Slowly, lasciviously, he licks his palm clean, fat pink tongue against fat white skin. He wipes away that stain.

He ended up with six sons, none of his own loins. Each had been deposited in his care by some easy or sassy or floozy woman who had mated with his partner, the Other Man, but who had no room or desire for the child. Each bastard had been a larger baby than the previous, and almost as if he had birthed them himself, the Fat Man also got heavier with each addition. And in the end, although he wanted to be proud like the other parents were proud, this fruit had not fallen far from the Other Man's tree. The Fat Man had raised beasts: two-legged animals with a strong criminal bent and no consideration for the rest of humankind. They had grown from screaming, discontented babies to angry, violent men, feet planted squarely in the footprint of their birth father.

He had raised six boys for this Other Man, each wilder than the last, each coming to rest further away from the norm. The bluntness of their intellect was equaled only by the sharpness of their aggressiveness, and they were a burden to everyone. One by one they left, and he was relieved. Three made their way to the mean streets of distant cities and two were lost in this wild countryside, unidentified bones found years after a drunken spree. The youngest, the one that had been a full thirteen pounds when he came to this house at two days old, dropped off by a woman with a frazzled blond wig, a dangling cigarette and too much lipstick, had not spoken until age five. When he did first speak, it was clear that he had been listening, at least to the Other Man. This one was a shard of that man's cold mirror. "Fat ass," he spat at the Fat Man as he tried to keep the child from eating scraps pulled from the kitchen garbage pail. "Leave me alone."

At seventeen, this youngest boy had been given a life sentence to the state prison for the violently ill. He'd killed the school lunch cook, beat her to death with a metal serving tray. She had refused to give him a third helping of cherry cobbler. When he continued to demand more – "I want more, you fuckin' bitch" – she called him a 'fat little bastard' and turned her back. He showed her. Before the police arrived to bind him in a straightjacket and drag him through the stunned lunchroom crowd, he had gobbled most of an industrial-sized cherry cobbler. No careful timing, no perfect world there.

The Fat Man hadn't objected to the boy's sentence; he was the last one to tie him to this unwanted brood of man-beasts. With the boys gone, he sat alone with their father in the middle of their shacks upon shacks, no children to answer to, and none to issue demands.

He hadn't objected to his sentence.

Discipline, he tells himself, is biting a tiny hole in the softened chocolate coating and sucking the liquid out slowly, with a bit of noise; a porcine slurping of the stale guts surrounding the cherry center. One pearlescent drop escapes his corpulent lips to rest squarely on the outcropping of his chin. He carefully wipes it with one finger, coaxing it back to his mouth, and swallows it loudly, greedily. And then, without chewing, he swallows the candied cherry heart whole, now loosely draped in shrunken, wrinkled, melting chocolate skin.

Those children were never a source of solace. None of them had taken after him; they all gravitated toward their father. Each was unmistakably the Other Man's spawn, crude pieces somehow broken from the original block: tall, hairy, thick-limbed, heavy-browed, animal-like, with his full lips and small, angry eyes.

When the Fat Man was twenty, the Other Man had appeared one Friday night at the concession counter of the local movie theater, where the Fat Man barely made enough money selling candies and sodas to pay for what he consumed. The Fat Man had taken scarce notice of the Other Man. When he returned the next week and asked him out – "Hey, big guy, wanna' go out?" – the "big guy" had found him only mildly attractive, agreeing to a date not so much because he liked the looks of the Other Man, or was even interested, but because offers of dinner had been few. There were not many men in these parts interested in other men, and the ones that were didn't want a fat guy.

While having this first meal together, the Fat Man noticed the way the suitor ate his food one item at a time: first the meatloaf, without a bite of anything else, until it was gone; then the mashed potatoes, again without interruption. Finally, he ate the peas, only not by the forkful, but one pea at a time. This order, in the Fat Man's life of disorder, was savory, and he began to warm to the Other Man. Later that evening, after the Other Man had screwed him from behind in the back seat of the Fat Man's mother's Plymouth, laughing and slapping his rotund ass the entire time as he likened the ride to that of the Hindenberg, the Fat Man began to think the other might be the one. But it wasn't until the first woman was already pregnant with the first of the boys, when the Other Man began to show up drunk for dates if he bothered to show up at all, that the Fat Man knew it was love. They moved in together shortly before the birth.

Order, he reasons, as he arranges the last five chocolates in a circle in the upturned lid of the candy box, is something he has only experienced from a distance, externally. Order is nothing more than knowing that darkness falls every night, and each year will bring another child and another 20 pounds. Order has never been graceful, never been pleasant. He stares at the circle of chocolates, barely visible in the dim moonlight, and contemplates the order in which he will eat them, exactly three minutes apart. He picks up the first one, warming it in his hand. After his wait, his untimed yet precise wait, he eats it, deliberately, and in exactly three bites.

Alone in the darkness, the last four chocolates like a constellation on his sagging lap, the Fat Man's mind turns to thoughts of the Other Man. He mumbles aloud the names he was called, repeating them to himself in a low, rumbling, sing-song voice. "Fatso, chubby, lardo, muley, moose. Fatso, chubby, lardo, muley, moose."

He remembers a summer night long ago, the two of them sitting in this room, the light of the television casting a glow, everything tinged in eerie blue. There is no sound, as if he has been deafened, as if all sound has been muted. He can feel the sound vibrating from the television, but he cannot hear it. Even the sounds he feels are somehow intangible, like what he is experiencing is the essence of sound, not the sound itself.

Through the odd blue light, through the muted silence, shines a harsh beacon light, the source of which is the Other Man, his partner, reclining in his chair – this very chair the Fat Man now sits in – clad in nothing but yellowed boxer shorts, illuminated by the pale light of the TV. And the beacon says, "Get off your fat ass and get my dinner."

He pops the next chocolate into his mouth, swirling it against the ridged roof with his cupped tongue, relishing the melted chocolate, slurping the viscous creamy juice between the shell and the cherry heart like it is cum, like he has just sucked the cock of the now-dead Other Man.

The Other Man always made the Fat Man swallow.

"Get off your ass if you aren't too god-damned fat."

The Fat Man never recognized the abuse. The names the Other Man called him were terms of endearment, things he said only to the Fat Man. They were his and only his. Here, on the edge of this run-down town, in this home built of huts, with those wild sons and that hateful Other Man, he had felt as though he belonged for the first time since childhood. Even after the disappointment and departure of those bastard sons, when it was just the two of them, he had belonged here, with the Other Man.

The Other Man died slowly and painfully, rotting from the inside, the cancer taking away his anger and his crudeness and all of the names he called the Fat Man, chewing away at his rancid core until nothing was left but the shell. He was a chocolate-covered cherry of a man with the juice slowly sucked out, the cherry gulped greedily. It was as if the Other Man's very meanness turned inward, ground him with its dentures, and swallowed. He left the Fat Man, and there was no longer anyone to tell him he was fat.

The Fat Man rearranges the three remaining chocolates in a smaller circle, and then eats one. Because he cannot make a circular pattern out of the last two, he quickly eats another. He justifies forgoing the three-minute rule because the rule of circles is stronger. Discipline, he thinks, is knowing when to eat the chocolate quickly.

He is left with one halo of chocolate-flavored paraffin encasing one curved cherry.

He recalls the full box of cherries, and this makes him think of the shack crowded with wild boys. He pictures the circle of five candies in the box lid on his lap; a circle made of spheres of chocolate-flavored paraffin encasing round cherries. Life imitates confection, and even a life as simple as his is somehow circular. Memories of the Other Man, dead, and his look-alike, act-alike sons, long gone, come to mind. Alone in the dark, his mass draping the recliner, he plays with the lone cherry. He picks it up and rolls it between his pink sausage fingers, and then carefully places it back in the lid of the empty box.

This is the last cherry. This cherry lingers.

He touches the glistening chocolate gently with one fleshy finger; its surface gives slightly. He presses harder, and when he releases he sees a perfect fingerprint shining back at him in the faint light.

In resignation, because the three minutes have been duly counted off, he picks up this last cherry and tosses it toward his gaping mouth. His moist tongue curls to catch the morsel, but this ornery bit of sweet misses its mark. Undisciplined and disorderly, it passes his waiting tongue, teeters at the back of his mouth, and then falls. It does not take the esophageal route, but turns to the trachea and promptly lodges in his airway. His throat tightens as his body involuntarily tries to force out a breath, one strong gasp to dislodge this intruder. But he has no air, he cannot exhale, and the soft, waxy cherry forms a complete and solid seal. Breathless, trapped, too tired and too heavy to get out of the chair, too weak to struggle, he experiences a gradually expanding sense of calm and peace. In death's warm embrace he begins to hallucinate, to travel backwards in his life.

He revisits that night in front of the television, when sound became a sensation and light was odd and blue, the same pallor as his current oxygen-deprived face. The light now flickers as the moonlight passes through the oily pane of the barren window, like that light from the television that night. The Fat Man's death memories intensify, become colorful, ever brighter and more vivid until he is awash in color, until he is the center of a dead universe from which vast swirls of color and memory emanate. Suddenly, as if the very weight of the mass of color and recollection becomes too much and can no longer support itself, this universe collapses. The color fades back to the blue light of the television, which shrinks to a distant pinpoint, and the Fat Man moves toward it. Without leaving the chair of his death, he follows the blue pinpoint to the horizon. When he reaches it the light again expands, and his field of vision broadens. In death, his vision is clear.

He is a child again, perhaps five years old, rosy-cheeked and chubby, slipping out of his warm childhood bed in the middle of the winter night, bare feet paddling like animal paws on the cool tiles of the floor. He has heard someone moving about in the lighted kitchen at the rear of the country house, but he is not afraid. He makes his way through the dark hallway toward the brightness. Standing at the entrance, blinking back the eye-stinging light reflecting from polished surfaces, he sees his father. Tall and lean, crisp in his square black overcoat and hat, he is placing his packed suitcase by the back door.

The Fat Boy is his father's son, the apple of his eye, and the fruit of his labor. Father is of German stock – prudent, ethical, hard-nosed and driven. He arrived on these shores a young man with old-world values, penniless but willing to work hard to assimilate. And he has, even to the point of taking an American wife when the time came to take a wife. He did not find (he did not even look for) a shy and subservient immigrant shepherd girl who tends to her husband as carefully as she tends to her flock. He took an American wife who nags at him constantly, nibbling away at his self-worth bite-by-bite, minute-by-minute, refusing in the end ever to be satisfied, even though he works harder than any man should to put food on their table.

No, this is not a marriage of love or even convenience. What is the convenience of constant turmoil? This marriage is an adjustment, a fine-tuning of his naturalization. A man reaches an age and takes a wife. If that wife helps him become a citizen of the land he tills, so much the better. The utility of the arrangement appeals to his well-developed sense of purpose. And from this marriage came a son, and the father loves him.

He loves him, but he is frugal with praise. At the Fat Boy's tender age, not yet pubescent, not yet even prepubescent, he has impressed on the boy his immigrant's value of hard work, of leading a disciplined and orderly life. In this God-fearing home, rigid with old-world morality, even the morning oatmeal – stirred with a careful measure of raw sugar – must be earned. For the boy, chores come before breakfast. For him, the early bird does not just get the worm; the early bird *earns* the worm.

But the boy loves his father. He adores him. He is his pillar. His love is the boy's just desserts. He can do no wrong. At night, in the darkness of his room, in the stillness and quiet, when he hears his mother and his father arguing – he cannot make out the words they utter, but he knows it is argument because he can recognize the hostility even in the hushed voices and he can feel the anger even without knowing why it is there – he always places blame with his mother. The father can do no wrong. He is his pillar; his love is the Fat Boy's dessert.

The father sees the boy now, trying to rub the sleep from his eyes with one fat fist of curled fingers, smiling at him. He moves to where the boy stands in the doorway, and bends stiffly at the waist until his face is level with the child's. Kissing him gently on the forehead, he whispers softly in his hair, in his ear.

"My plump little cherry, my love," he coos as best he can with his hard German accent, "be disciplined, be orderly, be all you can. Do not forget me." He slips a chocolate from his pocket to the boy's hand, stands once again straight and tall, and turns off the light. He leaves through the back door, suitcase in hand, disappearing into the deeper darkness of the countryside. It is the last time the Fat Boy will ever see him. He walks into the darkness and the silence, leaving his nagging wife, leaving his morality, leaving his precious Fat Boy and that delicious adoration.

For three full minutes the Fat Boy stands still and mute, waiting for the door to open, for father to return. But the door does not open; father does not return. Slowly, the Fat Boy sinks to the floor, chocolate melting in his hand. He is sitting in the darkness. Alone.

WALKING THE BLIND DOG

Dogs are our children, and my dog-child is blind.

The blind dog might tumble akimbo off a curb if my vigilance lapses (true fact – it happened once, accidentally, before I knew how to walk the blind dog and before she'd learned to walk as one).

Our outings demand my patience – we loiter more than walk. But she's old so I don't mind, and I keep it simple, taking the same turns every time. She's adept at mental mapping, having long ago mastered the la-la loft condo's layout. She has only once been terribly, temporarily skewed by an ill-conceived furniture rearrangement. Even then, dogpaddling at heaven's gate if one computes the usual canine to human conversions, she mapped anew. And now our walk has carved itself in her Shih Tzu memory.

She nose tests the elevator's door when it *dings* on our floor, then leaps in if nothing bumps. Eight downward *dings* later, we are deposited in the lobby. Outside, she immediately yanks toward the alleyway (right turn), following the tease of last night's catfish dinner special seeping from the café's dumpster. Here, she pees (copious and beer-yellow – been hours).

At V Street she turns left, where the concrete slabs have been tossed apart by the Herculean roots of a black walnut. They are a helter-skelter walkway and the blind dog must crawl, nose to ground, on point for the brown dirt-wood scent of a lifted or gapped stumbling block. Still, this is where she poops, always mid-sidewalk. She won't trust the more unreliable grass and soil, and she cares not whose curb appeal she defiles. No, she squats where the urge strikes and where the playfield is relatively level. I hover at the ready, right hand blue-bagged, to claim her warmth, staring apologetically at the lucky neighbor's home, especially when he sits on his porch – as the cat man often does.

Cat man: relic of the neighborhood pre-gentrification, revealed before seen, if the breeze is *just so*, by the stank of cigarettes and cat piss, which the dog ignores. She turns a deaf nose to him *and* the new folk buying up this refurbished block of reinforced windows.

We proceed east. Mid-block is where our local gang hangs out, more beautiful in their dangerous dark skin than is right. Also block remnants, they are what my father would have called "juvenile delinquents". Or worse. I try (successfully) not to make eye contact, and (unsuccessfully) not to inhale their fine male scent. I sense their disgust, hear one spit *old fag, retarded dog*. We move on. One day they will shoot me, everyone warns, but it doesn't keep me away.

The city's Art School lists above the next corner, tattered symbol of art's dwindling status. The dog turns left again (north on 13th Street), where the stones cobble underfoot. Here we listen to a joyous drum circle or flute or acting lesson (fighting or loving or fear) or the hammering and sawing of prop construction, with laughter, all of which I don't mind loitering through and all of which assures us, the blind dog and I, of art's real value.

On the next corner sits a chain-linked vacant lot, overgrown and very peed upon – even my human nose knows this is where all dogs leave their mark. Their urine is a calling card printed in the grammar of dog pee, which only dogs understand. The blind dog adds her note.

We turn left, west on W Street, where two crows and a starling trade insults over a tossed-off chicken bone. The crows are bigger but my money's on the starling, who bickers tenaciously. A sapling strangles itself in the rusted links. I snap a twig with leaves veined and raspy; they taste of bitter gum, which tells me they are elm. The stump end of the branch thup-thup-thups against the wire as I cajole the blind dog into moving along.

Between the pee lot and the condo stands another row of homes, these occupied by recent immigrants (taxi drivers, mostly) except for Mrs. Wu, the uprooted suburban gardener. Mrs. Wu, strongly encouraging socialization, shoves her timid Ping Pong (Shih Tzu, too) against the gate with a calloused foot. The dogs numbly exchange sniffs. I admire Mrs. Wu's tree peonies.

The starling flies overhead, chicken bone in hand (or more correctly, beak) as the blind dog, cued by the thwack-thwack of cars rattling over a loose manhole cover, pulls me left into our alley.

In the elevator I unleash, reward (butt scratch and/or belly rub) as she stares up at me, dead eyes eerily unfocused but on a happy face. We count the dings back up to eight.

AT THE SEX PARTY

I finished my fourth bourbon and Diet Coke as I watched the boy on the far side of the hotel lobby. I'd seen the young man yesterday, when I'd arrived at the Chicago Lakeside Hotel for my first-ever International Fetish Man convention. As I'd dragged my suitcase toward the registration counter – only Friday afternoon and already the hotel filled shoulder-to-shoulder with six-thousand raunch-minded gay men – I had felt adrift in a sea of leather and lust. In the khakis and blue polo shirt I had chosen for the flight from Washington, I might as well have been wearing a bridal gown. I'd known I needed to change into something more appropriate. Fast. And then I needed a drink. Or four.

As my room key had been activated and my credit card swiped, the boy had nuzzled a muscle bear's armpits at the far end of the registration counter. The big bear leaned against a wall, his hands clasped behind his head, eyes closed, as the boy first worked one side and then moved to the other, licking from the mountain of bicep down to the moist valley of pit.

The pretty girl taking my information had watched them, too. "Hot, huh?" she'd commented, surprising me.

"What does the hotel staff think of this?" I'd asked.

"This group is the first sold-out booking since this hotel was built in 1927, and you guys are great tippers. We're happy. That's why they've pretty much given you all free rein. The only thing we are instructed to stop in the public areas is, um," she giggled, "anal sex. Everything else, we don't say a word."

At the opposite end of the long counter, two young blond men who looked very much alike had dropped to their knees. They took turns stroking the large, frenum-pierced dick hanging from the fly of a dark man's white boxer shorts. His only other clothing was a pair of army boots. In short order his cum had dripped to the floor between them.

"My boss says we are making enough money to replace all the carpets if we have to," the clerk had added, nodding toward them. "And we might have to." She'd handed me my key card. "Room three-eighteen. Have fun, Mr. Foster."

I'd seen armpit boy several times since check in yesterday, but always in passing, and always when he was involved with some other guy. In the free-wheeling hubbub of all these fetish-loving men holed up in one hotel, I hadn't yet managed a face-to-face.

The boy was busy even now as I watched him, chatting up a man whose back was to me. But I'm a tenacious cock-blocker, a real pitbull when there's a bone I want. I stared. I would make certain the boy saw me this time. Sure enough, he finally glanced over his friend's shoulder. I nodded, the boy nodded back. I rubbed the swollen head of my cinched up dick through the worn denim of my jeans. The black snap-on cockring was doing a fine job of flaunting my best asset. The boy licked his lips.

In this gilded lobby, day two of this convention, it was a standard greeting.

But then the boy went back to his conversation. *I'll get to you later*, I thought, *the weekend is young*. There was plenty to keep me occupied until I caught up with that one. Like the two dudes to my immediate left, just inside the hotel's revolving door. One was a well-stacked Latino wearing chainmail shorts – and nothing else, unless you counted the silhouette of a longhorn's head, the eyes blazing red, tattooed across his chest. He kissed a stocky black guy in a yellow jockstrap. Their tongues flicked, pink on pink. They were making out just to the side of a sign the hotel's management had taped in the shuttered window: *"Due to the hotel being sold out for a private event, the facilities are closed to the public."*

Yellow Jockstrap squatted as urine drizzled from the heavy hang of Longhorn's chainmail. He lapped, missed nary a drop. The pink flicking continued, only now the tongue danced with chrome links and pale yellow beer piss. Even though watersports weren't on my wish list, I kept watching. They needed an audience; I hated to disappoint.

The show was interrupted when a hand gently stroked the small of my back. The boy from across the lobby had found his way over.

"Hey," I said. The boy's palm, the touch softer and lighter than I had imagined, slid up the length of my shirtless back and came to rest on my shoulder. "Hey," he replied. I pulled him in for a kiss.

More standard greeting.

The boy's mouth tasted of vodka and other men, and his thick black moustache smelled of someone else's crotch. I sniffed, and ran my tongue along his teeth. He responded by shoving a thick wad of spit into my mouth. Then he pulled away. I swallowed the gift and wiped my wet chin with the back of a hand.

"I'm Antonio," the boy said. The accent was Brooklyn. "Sex party, room ten-oh-eight. Follow me."

"Bennett Foster," I replied. And then I followed him.

When two – or more – men hook up for sex, during the trip from wherever they met to wherever they plan to fuck, they carry themselves as though they aren't together. There is no chitchat as a man drags a guy to his bathhouse cubicle or the backroom of some dank bar. Or to a sex party on the tenth floor. One silently shadows the other to the steamy destination, like it's 1952 and such things must still be kept secret. For all of our freedoms, our declarations, when it comes right down to it gay men often still move in the shadows. At least when we are making naughty moves.

The elevator going up to the tenth floor was no exception. Antonio took a stance on one side, I leaned against the other. There was no chatter. Instead, we examined the elegant rosewood paneling, the strung-crystal chandelier that shimmied as we bumped past each floor. We watched the CNN Headline news displayed on the tiny elevator television. Murders had risen by a quarter in Detroit, a clean-cut anchor explained. I knew with full certainty that the reporter didn't have a codpiece and harness tucked under that pinstriped suit, was not enjoying a vibrating butt plug below the sterile anchor's desk. "The stock market rallied today," the anchor continued.

I looked for an off button; there wasn't one.

When the doors parted on ten, I stayed in Antonio's wake. Our boot-clad feet clomp-clomped in rhythm, a steady drumbeat along the beige-carpeted hallway. Laughter bubbled out of some rooms; moans and obscenities out of others.

I watched the "V" of Antonio's back, the shape emphasized by the snug latex vest that zipped up one side. Between the vest's bottom edge and the low-riding waistband of Antonio's Levi's, the upper part of his ass was on display. A mounded hump pulsed on each side of the cleft; black curls, damp, lined it.

My burning stare must have warmed it; Antonio didn't miss a step as he ran the middle finger of his right hand down the slit, well into the nether land. Still walking down the long hallway, he pointed the digit back at me, face-level. I sniffed, I licked. The scent was fecund, the flavor metallic.

The sentry posted outside room ten-oh-eight wore black knee-height boots and loose-fitting, unbuttoned jeans *almost* held in place by black leather suspenders. He looked at Antonio and me, nodded, and then pulled a key card from his back pocket. The mechanism whirred and clicked, and the door opened when he turned the latch. I followed Antonio in.

In the dim lighting – the room illuminated only by what glare escaped from the two inches the bathroom door was cracked – I saw a standard setup: two queen beds with nightstands, a small desk and chair, an armoire. What weren't standard were the fifty-or-so men in various states of undress, humping in every available space, in every imaginable position. The prohibition on fucking met its end in ten-oh-eight.

Sound – slapping, slurping, hushed whispers, a steady thump-thump-thumping – came from all around, yet an odd quiet persevered. No one spoke in a normal tone. The rank, dirty-sock smell of poppers and sweat and cum left no room for conversation. It barely left room for oxygen. I thought of waterfalls, how sometimes the sound deafens, yet remains distant and undefined, a very quiet kind of loud.

Antonio unzipped his vest and jeans, and bent over to unlace his boots. I did the same, and when we came face to face again, our naked bodies met. As we kissed, other hands reached from the darkness toward us, caressing, pulling, and probing. Someone handed Antonio a bottle of poppers. He closed one nostril with the thumb of the hand holding the bottle, aligned the opening beneath the other nostril, and inhaled deeply. He repeated on the other side and then handed the bottle to me. I did my own double shot and then passed the bottle on.

All sensation amplified. The hands touching me heated, caressed more passionately. My body responded, moved in the darkness toward the stimulation, sought touch. Antonio kissed me; his tongue darted into my mouth. I moaned, flushed simultaneously hot and cold. An overwhelming sensual brightness generated from just behind my closed eyelids. I swayed in place, felt as good as one can ever expect to feel. Perhaps even better.

When I opened my eyes; Antonio had turned his back. He bent at the waist, inhaled from the popper bottle again, and gently wagged his ass at my dick. He spat in his own hand, reached around, and lubricated my shaft. He backed up; I moved forward. Contact, then I slid in. Together we swayed. The bottle of poppers came again and again, the two of us huffing and fucking like the man-sex pros we were. We didn't miss a beat, didn't spill a drop of the skin-blistering liquid as the frantic pounding together of our bodies joined the cacophony of sound in the room. Faster and faster we fucked until, in a popper-induced starburst, we both came.

My cock slid out as we parted. In the low light it glistened, flaccid, wet with cum and ass moisture. Antonio righted himself and we kissed. We held each other, strong fingers stroking the length of each other's backs, bristled cheeks nestling. Our racing hearts slowed together. It was the usual gay male after-sex cuddling. Always, even if only briefly, we share a moment of intimacy afterwards. Maybe it's to make up for the shadow slinking; maybe it's just a human need for psychic contact. Or maybe we are just more wired for afterplay than foreplay.

For the first time since we left the lobby, Antonio spoke. "So," he whispered, "I guess I should have asked about your status." I was surprised: one could hear a Brooklyn accent even in a whisper.

"I have a boyfriend, but we have an open relationship," I replied. "I left him at home."

"No, I mean . . . you know. *Status*. Health."

I laughed, even though nothing was funny. I gave an open-armed shrug, both palms up.

"Look where we are," I said, gesturing to the men still humping around us, not a condom in the room. Antonio looked around, then back at me, puzzled.

"Who would bareback if they were negative?" I asked.

Antonio stared for a minute, slack-jawed. The sparkle of a tear slid down the right side of his face.

"Oh, fuck," I whispered. "I just assumed you were poz, too."

"It was bound to happen," Antonio choked out. "My mistake. I assumed you weren't."

"I should have said something. I just assumed."

"My mistake," Antonio said, again. "Heat of the moment . . . the poppers . . . it was bound to happen. Sooner or later."

The moon surely stopped rising over Lake Michigan, the night hawks had to have become still in the blue-black sky. There weren't fifty men fucking within touching distance. There was nothing but a boy from Brooklyn and me, regretting together. Another tear streaked down Antonio's face, and in the next heartbeat, mine flowed. Like waterfalls, I thought again. Instinctively, we held each other. Just as instinctively, the hands reaching for us in the darkness fell away.

"We're crying at a sex party," I murmured. "I'm sure there are rules against that."

"Probably," Antonio sniffed. But we continued to hug, to cry, to whisper in the dark. We wept ourselves dry, agreed to stay in touch, to be more responsible, to share the guilt for what had just happened. Finally there was nothing else to be said, nothing more to be done except put on our jeans and our leathers. We exchanged phone numbers and readied to emerge from ten-oh-eight.

As we clutched each other one last time, the latex of Antonio's vest now cold against my sex-dampened skin, a voice penetrated our shared penitence. Someone had finally spoken aloud – it was one of the men on the bed behind us. He spoke roughly to his partner-of-the-moment.

"Yeah, take it. Take it. I'm gonna give it to you."

"That is really not what I need to hear right now," I whispered. Antonio nodded in agreement. We left, Antonio turning right in the hallway as I turned left.

During the solitary elevator back down to my room, the CNN broadcast had looped full circle. "Murders have risen by a quarter in Detroit," the handsome anchor repeated.

"In Chicago," I whispered, mimicking him, "HIV infections have risen by one."

DOSE OF REALITY

Before it turned in to a pile of steaming, um, *rubble*, the winter of 1993 had been fabulous – everything a young gay man could hope for. Credit love. And sex. Mind-blowing sex with a guy who was almost my perfect match. Almost. We *were* serodisconcordant. He was HIV-positive, I was HIV-negative. But that detail seemed surmountable; just keep "it" under wraps when sir's doing the mounting. Easy-breezy.

But then, during one particularly athletic sexcapade, a little more than my mind was blown. The shredded condom, flapping on its pole like the enemy army's flag planted on my horizon, proclaimed loud and clear that I'd been invaded. Talk about a party stopper. I tried laughing it off, hoped for the best, but I knew that my body – the traitor – had never met a virus it didn't welcome with wide-open antibodies. From whooping cough to chicken pox to measles to Hepatitis A, it had spent a lifetime practicing non-discrimination. And true to form, within the year my ELISA HIV-antibody test results changed from negative to positive.

It's a preliminary test, I reminded myself, prone to inaccuracies and false-positives. The follow-up Western Blot test, the most accurate in those days (and the most expensive which explains why my insurance carrier restricted it to cases of confirmation only), *might* come back with different results. But from my deepest heart of hearts, that rational voice I so rarely paid any mind niggled: *You should prepare for the possibility that it's positive.*

I took this to mean I should immediately begin to obsess about dying. So I did. Mightily.

But mostly, for the two endless weeks it took for the test results to come back, I ruminated about the two possible outcomes: condemnation or . . . *fingers crossed and Jesus, I promise, I swear on my Granny's good name, I will never again do anything even remotely exciting, no matter how unbelievably hunky a man is, if you'll just let me slide this one little time . . .* salvation. Come judgment day, I would either thank my very fortunate stars, feeling positive about maintaining a negative status, or, fall devastated to the lowest low, positively negative about having converting to positive.

Wait . . . what?

I couldn't make sense of the language, let alone the implications. It was all so confusing that it was actually a relief when the results finally came in – at least I knew where I stood. Unfortunately, I stood squarely on the side of tainted. *This is it*, I thought: *this is my defining moment, and it isn't a definition I like.*

An HIV infection in the early 90's was essentially a terminal diagnosis. The single available treatment was AZT, a nucleoside analog reverse transcriptase inhibitor, or nuke.

Isn't *that* cute?

But this little nuke had two problems. First, it was not very functional. It worked only in some cases, and often only for a short while. Secondly, it destroyed the man as much as the virus. Not a pleasant option. My trusted physician, Dr. Peter, advised me that more effective treatments were just around the corner and, since my "numbers" were thus far "non-threatening", we might consider waiting to begin treatment.

Numbers; too many numbers to count. There were viral loads and CD4 counts and milligrams and parts per liter and parts per million and acceptable ratios and percentages and . . . oh, man – why hadn't I paid attention in even the most rudimentary of math classes? My high school teachers had warned that I would need algebra in real life; I had no idea this was what they meant. My viral load and CD4 count might not yet be threatening, but this numbers thing certainly was.

Dr. Peter channeled the patience of Saint Peter as he explained to me the ins and outs, the norms and not-so-norms, of my diagnosis. He produced several kindergarten-worthy diagrams in pretty pastel colors that illustrated the probable progression of the disease. We could wait until the rising pink line crossed the dipping turquoise line to start treatment, he counseled, but no longer. Together, Dr. Peter and I decided to postpone chemical intervention until the proper numbers did a nose dive – or was it a sudden spike? – and/or until more effective and tolerable medications were available.

But I couldn't just sit on my thumbs and do *nothing*, so I did what any rational person in my situation would do. I wrote a florid self-obituary, doled my prized possessions out to stunned friends, stopped paying my credit card bills (but didn't stop charging things), and gave up making plans beyond the upcoming weekend. And I waited for the grim reaper's certain appearance. I fine-tuned those new death-obsession skills, scrambling to Dr. Peter's office with every sniffle and pimple. Was this *it*?

There is no horror movie that can produce the fear I felt in Dr. Peter's waiting room. A cadre of walking skeletons and living zombies were propped on the unattractive mauve office furniture, their death masks contorted in various stages of withered pain. It seemed as though I peered through a twisted, fast-forward Alex-in-Wonderland looking glass, and what I saw on the other side was my immediate and unnatural demise. This was my unavoidable future, a scenario rendered crystal clear by the AIDS-related death of the lover who infected me – succumbed to a type of cancer that normally afflicted people twice his age.

Until I seroconverted, Dr. Peter had been little more than my peter doctor, *tsk-tsking* like a much cuter and way-more-gay Marcus Welby while dispensing medications for the occasional bout of common gonorrhea or crabs. A quick shot or a stinging shampoo and I was cured. Like a ham.

Oh, how I longed for the good old days, but they were no more.

Dr. Peter suggested I start on Crixivan, the eighth FDA-approved antiretroviral and the first approved protease inhibitor, when my viral load climbed to over 50,000 RNA copies per milliliter of blood plasma. Are you getting a sense of the complexity of the numbers game yet? Don't worry, I never got it, either. All I knew was my number was up.

In order to get my insurance provider to pay for the Crixivan, still considered experimental at that point, I had to agree to meet regularly with their Case Manager, a perky young woman who spoke in cheerful platitudes about every dark cloud's silver lining and all bad paths leading to a new fork in the road. All the while she kept more than a respectable distance between us and repeatedly washed her hands. I wanted to put a fork in her forehead.

Crixivan was the first medication ever prescribed to me without a stop date, and it was not a gentle deflowering. Crixivan requires three doses spread evenly over the day's 24 hours. Not ten minutes before or after the scheduled dose, but on the mark. And that target has to be one hour before or two hours after a meal. Again, no room for variance.

Eating devolved from a lovely leisure activity to a rigorously timed obstacle course. If there were an Olympic event for eating on schedule, I would be a gold medalist. I am the Michael Phelps of scheduled eating.

My social life took careful reconnaissance. Have you ever tried to gracefully beg out of a five course gourmet dinner lovingly prepared by a Food Network devotee? Without divulging your HIV status? Not only was I learning how to maintain an unyielding medication regimen, something that has proved useful in later years, I was developing some pretty sharp manipulation skills. Come to think of it, those have come in handy, too.

The thing about Crixivan is that it often stops working. Most people get another year or two out of it before their numbers again start herding them toward the grave. So I took my pills on schedule but continued waiting for death. But the unforeseen happened. I lived. And kept living. New drugs were developed; eventually the HIV medication regimen became more efficient and less dramatic. I was even forced to start paying those credit card bills again (but I never did manage to re-collect all my keepsakes).

These days I take three medications for my HIV infection – a drug cocktail, perhaps the most boring cocktail I've ever had – in the form of two tablets once a day. And when I visit Dr. Peter, the men waiting with me are unremarkable: a fairly normal bunch of aging baby boomer queens. If there is a death bed candidate in the group it is likely due to prostate cancer or a brain aneurysm or multiple myeloma. Nowadays, when HIV infection is detected early and treated appropriately, nearly every clinical problem associated with it has become something less than critical. As Dr. Peter recently said, "We don't look at this as an acute and terminal illness any longer; we view it like diabetes, a chronic but treatable condition. It's manageable."

For anyone who thinks that this statement justifies relaxing safe sex protocols, let me remind you that as of 2012, upwards of 15,000 people die annually from AIDS-related illnesses in the United States, and the numbers – damn those persistent numbers – are much higher in less developed countries. But here in the western world at least, while still presenting significant social, economic, and cultural problems, AIDS is no longer an automatic death sentence. I was surprised recently when I did my own math (on a calculator, of course – some things, like math skills, never get better): I've been managing *it* for 19 years now.

Managing, yes, but not forgetting. HIV infection is still a significant influence, one that shades all of my days. But I have come to realize is that I am not defined by this infection. I am defined by how well I live with it.

I'm no longer a young man. A few years ago my physical examination revealed a cholesterol count of two-eighty-five with an HDL ratio of six. Forget dying of AIDS; a heart attack loomed with bleak certainty. The cure? No more red meat. Reject eggs. Don't even think about cheddar. Replace them with cardiovascular exercise, oats, and two white oval pills every morning. My risk was reduced, as were (again!) culinary joy and precious time spent sprawled on the sofa.

Then my blood pressure lifted off, orbited at one-seventy-two over one hundred. I blamed the exercise. This problem required two oblong blue tablets twice a day. Salt became a four-letter word. My pressure lowered, but my head spun faster, higher than a cyclone.

"Just a side effect," Dr. Peter explained.

"Seems less *side* than *central*," I replied. But I gag down the prescribed pink and white caplet each day as a countermeasure.

Still, time continues to hobble along. As my age increases, so do my weight and the number of medications I consume. Meanwhile, my platelets, range of motion, lung capacity, memory, libido, and hairline all dwindle. Dr. Peter adds Feretab, Flexeril, Albuterol, Rivastigmine, Testosterone gel, Viagra, and Propecia. Once a day, twice a day, every six hours, evening only, take with food, call your

136

doctor if an erection lasts longer than four hours, avoid grapefruit, may cause sleep disturbance. Add Ambien. This chemical panoply is quite a routine, yet, somehow, in no way compares to the strangling rigors of Crixivan. I remain oddly thankful for my early training.

The poignant fact here is that none of my conditions are HIV-related; they are all natural circumstances, manifestations of the human body's gradual demise. A situation which, I remind myself daily, was not always a probability for me. There was a time not so long ago when I knew with absolute certainty that I would not reach this age.

But no more. Dr. Peter will keep me going to eighty or ninety. Even beyond. I am the born again, the risen. Dr. Peter and I thwarted my early termination and now I will live out a just and golden decline. It is my divine privilege to do a long, slow dance with what summarily killed my peers, my lover, my friends. My aging bones shuffle to a melody as synthetic as the medications that sustain me, yet still it is a melody that brings joy to my heart and thankfulness to my every moment.

I have survived to die as nature intended.

NATURAL SELECTION

The rigid wooden slats of the park bench press relentlessly into my goose-pimpled back. A stocking cap rides low over my ears and most of my forehead, and a wool blanket – cocooned around my prone body – laps over my chin and tucks snugly around the sides of my face. Only my eyes, nose, and weather-cracked lips brave the raw chill. I gaze skyward as the frozen minutes slowly pass. I wouldn't normally choose to rest here in the dead of winter, but tonight I didn't have a choice. In life you are either a have or a have-not. Mike and I are have-not's.

The arctic air mass stalled over the city is colder than hell, I think, and with this thought a snort escapes my chattering teeth: how cold is hell, anyway? The damp sound rises as mist in the frigid night, swirling lighter than feathers in the stillness above. But this remnant of warmth quickly freezes and two tiny ice crystals – all that remain of the moisture – fall back to my ashy face, an amusing pinprick of sensation on my cold-deadened skin. I blow another breath through shivering lips, and this plume goes higher than the first but just as quickly disappears. No ice crystals tickle my face this time, though. They are vaporized by the dry, subzero night before they can fall the longer distance back.

This January darkness is as still as death and except for Mike and me, the graveyard quiet of the inner-city park opens only to an eerie emptiness. I like the serenity. Soon enough this crossroads will be busy – at sunrise these grounds shake off the bitter night's hibernation and rumble to life as a parade of characters trample through.

The homeless who spent the night at the shelters show up first. They are kicked out of their cots at 7:00 a.m. and don't have anywhere to go. So they park on these benches and wait for the eager, winter-wrapped tour groups who come to snap photos of the famous marble fountain standing watch over these glacial gardens. The down-and-out will ask the well-off to part with their spare change (like the bums know anything about spare change; when you have only pennies, nothing is spare).

The beggars ignore the workers who cross this square as a short cut to their downtown cubicles just a few blocks away. These upwardly-mobile professionals sport the season's most expensive trends; we *know* where their spare change goes. They scurry by in furs and topcoats, steaming espressos and cappuccinos warming polished nails through leather gloves, fresh-scrubbed faces glowing pink from the nip of frost. Makes me sick. But they don't like me, either. These locals see me every day. I am urban blight and they like to pretend I don't exist. I am simply something to be stepped around on the way to kiss the man's ass for the dollar. Like dog shit.

But that all happens later. Right now, not even the rats are out. This cold snap shatters all records and the rats have enough sense to stay in their dens. But since Mike and I wander den-less, we end up lying head-to-head on this bench, the fuzz of our wool caps just touching. Mike's blanket covers his face, and he sleeps, only God knows how. The uncomfortable wooden benches preclude snuggling and my blanket only partially fends off the killing frost. Besides, I am still high from the crack cocaine. So I shiver and fidget beneath the cover, too cold and too agitated to sleep.

Mike and I can't stay at the shelters, you see. Besides not being allowed to sleep with each other, their drug ban stops us cold. Those are rules we can't live by. The fit survive, though, and sometimes being fit means being resourceful. Mike and I survive hunkered in the shack we built of salvaged cardboard and stolen tarps. Tucked between the backside of an empty office building and a vibrating HVAC unit, our castle is no Hilton but it works. We stay warm and dry and we answer only to ourselves. Each night when the drug rush fades and sleep creeps in to take her place, Mike and I spoon side-by-side in our bed of wool blankets and harvest each other's warmth of body and spirit. Our toasty little shack radiates with the comforts of home.

"How's the weather?" Mike asks every night, snickering like a schoolgirl. He likes this ritual. For Mike, habit replaces the usual securities.

"Clear and still," I reply. "Clear up to your ass and still snowin'."

But tonight's story reads differently; ritual took a hit earlier. We returned to our alley shack after a day of scratching for a living on the streets to find only open sky above and hard asphalt below. The building's owner inspected his grounds and when he found our shanty, he hauled it off as trash. He couldn't see that the propped cardboard walls and pitched blue roof were shelter; he couldn't imagine that the banged-up red cooler and odds-and-ends dishes were a kitchen, or the layers of rugs and cardboard were a mattress. One man's home is another man's . . . junk.

I am sure he found pleasure in destroying our camp. In my outrage I can imagine him throwing the last pieces of it – a half-eaten can of stew and the cracked mirror we hung for decoration – to the top of the heaped dump truck. He curses, "Fucking waste products," as he wipes his hands of us.

"Look at that," I say, "the fucker left our blankets." They are wadded in a heap on the top of the HVAC unit. A kind gesture, but again, maybe he just forgot to throw them away.

"God dammit!" We swear together.

"What are we gonna' do?" Mike finally asks. I don't like the fear I hear in his voice.

"Fuck!" I yell. "Fuck. Fuck. Fuck."

I kick the humming HVAC unit. I need a rock.

A fat man sits in his idling BMW at the intersection of 20th and P Streets. The car's heater runs at full blast to keep the wind-chill at bay. The trash-littered corner hosts a busy Burger King, whose customers we ask to part with their change. Many do. They can't just brush us off with a guilty "don't have any". We watch through the storefront windows; we have seen the cashier drop coins to their cupped palms. We know they have change, and they know we know. This transparency works in our favor, and our funds accumulate. So it is here the fat man loiters, holding what we buy with the money we scavenge.

His name is Alvarado, and he is always eating, always wiping grease or oil or mayonnaise from his fat fingers and fat lips but never quite getting them clean, always smacking or swallowing as the next customer ambles toward the car (all trying to look like they aren't doing anything illegal). Alvarado is like an overweight, slick eagle. He has a pointed, hawkish nose and shiny black hair that he smoothes back with thick hair wax. His bird-like eyes are cunning, always searching, always on the lookout. Until he spots a sale, and then he can't be distracted.

Alvarado is a business man with good business sense, but his heart is no damn bigger or softer than the hard little bits of crack he sells us. He takes our panhandled pennies and nickels and turns them into a nice living. It doesn't matter that we deposit our coins with him rather than eat. He's only a supplier, he says, in a land where the natural order of supply and demand sets the course. People make their own choices, Alvarado says.

I give him the last of our money and he gives us a rock. He retreats behind the tinted windows of his warm car while we walk through the cold to the basement entrance on the backside of a building just off the busy corner. We're below street level, enclosed in the concrete box at the bottom of a flight of cement stairs, tucked away from the wind and relatively hidden from sight. We use this pit often, and so do the other crackheads in the neighborhood. Sometimes in the summer we have to wait up top with the shady-looking group loitering on the sidewalk, trying not to look like we are loitering, as we take turns in the secluded space below.

But not tonight. Tonight Mike and I have the joint to ourselves.

Spindly, leafless crepe myrtle branches drape across the open top, a natural ceiling that encloses the box. The spent blooms – in August they hung in brilliant pink bunches – lie in crunchy frozen brown piles in the dank corners of this cell, lumped with hundreds of burnt matches and nearly as many bits of plastic and paper that used to wrap our drugs. Even in the blast of clean, winter-fresh air, the rancid stench in this hole lingers: fetid, but strangely sweet. The odors of the frozen flowers, urine, and drug smoke mingle in the frostiness.

I watch as Mike pisses in the corner, his back to me and his squat shape straddling the steaming puddle of his urine. His barrel-chested torso sprouts thick, short arms – like stubby wings – and abbreviated, unbending legs that cause him to move with a jerking, penguin-like shuffle, almost a hop from one foot to the other. These shrunken arms and legs are the remnants of a childhood ailment and have set him apart ever since. I wonder how he survived on the streets before we found each other, but when he turns toward me and his open face shines in the dim light, I understand.

Mike's dumb innocence provides for him, for both of us really. It's like he hails from a different place, accidentally cast out of some higher reality to find shelter in this underworld. There is a goodness that dwells in Mike. Innate goodness. He even refuses to use the cardboard sign I give him that reads: *Please help, diabetic.* He would rather do without than deceive.

"It's not true," Mike says of my crude, hand-lettered sign. "I can't do that. That's lying."

I swear at him but I also make a different sign, and for this Mike thanks me. But I don't care either way. *Please help, disabled and hungry* works just as well and the coins accumulate.

Intellect bypassed Mike. It skirted right past his soft brown eyes and wide, easy grin. Instead of smarts, Mike glows with naïve good-heartedness – the same now as when I met him in rehab seven years ago. It was love at first sight, and we have been together ever since. Not that we call it love: street life is too hard for that. We're already black, drug-addicted, and homeless. That's three strikes. No need to add another layer of hate to the game. Besides, it's nobody's business what we do with each other. So we keep our bond secret. Mike and I know we are a duo and that's enough. What we have works. Our prey responds better to Mike's quiet stillness than my nervous agitation. I scare them. But I keep our predators at bay. I take care of Mike in a world that might beat him down, and his good nature keeps me human.

I put the larger half of the rock in a small brass pipe and tuck the leftover piece in the front pocket of my jeans. "Save this for later," I reason. "We'll be glad to have it then."

I light up first and suck the sweet, hot smoke deep into my lungs. I thwart the pressing cough with clamped lips and a willed refusal to let my chest tighten, and pass the pipe to Mike. He inhales and passes it back to me. We hold each smoke-filled breath as long as we can, passing the pipe back and forth until smoke stops and the dry, lifeless ash blows away on the icy breeze. And then we ride the wave of the high, floating away from the urine-soaked concrete on sturdy wings of smoke. Even the crepe myrtle seems to have a sudden flash of life; the barren branches shiver, as if in anticipation.

"I'm flyin' man, I'm fuckin' soarin'. Nothing compares, man, nothing fuckin' compares," I say. I put my hand in my pocket and roll the little bit of crack cocaine between my fingers. I can live as long as I can feel that.

Later we make our way through deserted streets to this park, wrap as best we can in our blankets, and ready for the long night ahead. We have nowhere else to go. I'm still high and in that warm glow I can ignore the cold-tingling of my toes and fingers. I stay awake through the night chattering about all kinds of bullshit but Mike is quiet.

Eventually the sun rises but day breaks freaky and slow. The sky gradually changes from the weird, bright black of the winter night to a dull grey, and then a pale light spreads over the grounds. Next thing you know, the sun pops up.

The fountain looms to my right, towering over the ice-bound gardens. A tourist once told me what the three white marble figures sharing the center column symbolize, but I can't remember exactly. The one looking out at me now may represent the seas. The chiseled marble man hoists a small sailboat in one hand and he pets a seagull with the other, but I appreciate his muscles more than I appreciate the art or the symbolism. In fact, I laugh.

"Fuckin' gulls," I swear, "flyin' fuckin' rats. Gull shit everywhere. Hate fuckin' gulls, Mike, don't you?"

Mike doesn't answer.

The early birds have been discharged from the shelters and take their place on the open benches. The first of the walking commuters begin to filter through as the traffic noise from outside the square grows louder. Another day unfolds but Mike and I stay put. The sun might be up but not the temperature, and the long night has drilled the chill to our very core. It will take time to thaw.

A flock of pigeons abandons its roost to search for breakfast on the sidewalks circling the fountain. After a moment they take to flight again, all of them lifting as one to make looping, playful patterns in the sky. They are stretching, waking up. They rise over the park and swing left and right, the nearly horizontal rays of the low morning sun flashing white on their bellies as they turn together, changing from dark shadows to white sparkles as they circle. They are like a school of fish darting effortlessly, fluidly, in the cold blue ocean of sky above. These pigeon-fish paint a beautiful picture across the ocean-sky, but I am the only one looking up.

And then just as suddenly as they rose the birds return to the ground – a flock acting with single-minded will – to scratch out a living on these streets. I check my pocket for a crumb to toss them, but the cupboard is bare except for the tiny bit of drug.

"Sorry, little fuckers," I say, "you don't get this."

Maybe I said something wrong because suddenly they all jump to the air, every single one of them, their wingtips slapping together at the bottom of each down stroke as they shove off. Every bird makes the same sound – *whap-whap-whap-whap-whap* – and as a flock they raise quite a ruckus. Sounds like people clapping for a show.

Flapping feathered bodies surround me, but they are different this time. The pigeons are scared, not playful, and when I see a bigger shape among them I know why. It's a falcon, and before I can do anything he has grabbed one pigeon in midair – just a few feet after takeoff – and slammed her back to the frozen earth, her plump body grasped in his sharp talons. She struggles for just a second but the falcon places two accurate pecks at her head and she stops wriggling.

No one else notices the fight. The workers power walk toward their careers, breaths like puffs of exhaust from their revved-up engines churning-churning-churning at full throttle, while the beggars sit idle, waiting for the busses to disgorge the tourist class who might, if luck prevails, offer up enough spare change to grant another day's survival. The birds are so far out of everyone's routine that they don't exist.

The falcon lifts off on strong, silent wings, dead pigeon swinging from one hooked claw. He lands in a sycamore tree and begins to pluck the pigeon. He's an expert plucker and feathers soon float on the breeze like snowflakes, falling on Mike and me, falling over the people walking. A woman brushes white down from her raven hair, but still doesn't notice the death story in the bare branches above. As she walks onward the dead pigeon's plumage drifts silently over the brittle yellow grass of winter.

The falcon finishes plucking and lifts his head above the naked corpse, his open beak addressing the cold white sky. He screams an eerie victory screech, but I don't know for whom he yells. Doesn't matter: I'm the only one who hears him, so I guess he cries for me.

"Jesus, Mike, do you see this shit? Fucker got him some breakfast."

Mike does not stir under his blanket, so I sit up and put the last of the rock in the pipe. My back aches from hours pressed against the hard bench and the movement pains me, but this spectacle of nature – so out of place in this urban setting – demands an audience. Besides, it's a wake and bake morning and although I know I should share with Mike, snoozers lose and we only have half a rock. I light the pipe and watch the falcon rip and swallow strips of flesh from the pigeon as I inhale the smoke. When I have finished I tap the ash from the pipe and return it to my pocket. Time to move on. I lean over and jab Mike with a sharp elbow. But he doesn't move.

"Wake up, fool," I say, as I pull the blanket away from his face.

Right off I know he is dead. From the looks of him, he's been dead most of the night. His eyes are open but crystallized, frozen solid. They are like mud puddle ice: shiny and reflective but cut through with the crisscrossed cracks that come with freezing. In their surface I see a distorted, broken-mirror reflection of the sky above. In Mike's frost-nipped eyes, the morning splinters and the shards don't line up at the edges. Broken pieces of cloud float across one eye and in the other I see the branch of a tree cutting a jagged gash across the blue sky. On this branch rests the half-eaten body of the pigeon, shreds of blood-red meat hanging in strings from her thin white bones. Her still-feathered head dangles, red eyes open but lifeless, a death cry strangled in her gaping beak. The falcon sits beside her, wiping the blood from his face on the rough wood of the branch between his feet.

The walking workers walk, the begging homeless beg. The tourists tour with their cameras ready. Horns honk and drivers drive in the traffic mess beyond the borders of this park.

I pull Mike's blanket back over his face.

"Fuckin' falcon," I mutter to myself. "Fuckin' everything," I continue, as a well-dressed tourist steps aside to avoid me.

"Hey, lady, spare some change for coffee?" I say. I must not scare her too badly, or maybe just enough. After she spills her pocket in my outstretched hand, I walk away.

"Fuckin' falcon," I repeat.

EIPILOGUE

A Y, ¡CARAMBA!, PAPI

The Happy Hour air is funked up - too many bodies in the bar.
And I am repeatedly jostled by boys hustling between their cliques and
the bartender. Other than this unintentional drink-fetching frottage I
am ignored, an old fish out of water in this gathering of barely-legal
gay spawn. A passing lad's elbow knocks against me, a dollop of his
brimming Cape Cod splashes across the out-of-fashion white canvas of
my left shoe. There is no apology as he skitters away. I whisper a curse
and wipe the splatter as best I can, and then stare at my wet, pink foot.
When I lift my gaze back to the melee, *he* fills the frame.

"*Ay ¡caramba!, Papi*," he says. "You are *muy bonito* for an
older man."

I often forget my age, am startled by the grizzled coot I see in
the mirror, so I wonder who the lucky recipient of this *molé*

compliment is. But when his twenty-year-young fingers graze my arm and linger, *yo comprendo*.

Such a pretty one, with ridiculous black eyelashes and perfect teeth tucked behind mounded pink lips. His *moreno* skin begs to be stroked, his startling *medianoche* hair is so brilliant the lush seems an afterthought. I am crushed by his bone structure, drilled by his dark eyes, sniffed out by his classic equine nose. His wide shoulders taper to a trim waist; twin globes of *pelo* counterweight the Latino muscle stacked above. He is *el guapito*: a warm spring breeze, crunching fall leaves, the sheen of a fresh December snow all rolled into one fine man.

Ay ¡caramba!, indeed.

Then Reality (who invited him?) reminds me that I'm likely older than *el padre del niño*, that I've circled this block more than once and swore to never again fall for some boy's *caca*. Reality has a prosecutor's persuasive skills. But the real reason I want to give this *chico* a stern talking to is his dredging up of age when he could have said I was handsome – period. Before I can unleash my tongue, though, *mi hijo* winks and says, "I only hope I end up as gorgeous as you."

His touch still burns a slow, beautiful hole in my arm, and I realize I don't really mind him using the "O" word. In fact, following with the "G" word pretty much cancels it out. I soak up his *azucarado* compliment. It drizzles into me, honey on a warm *sopapilla*.

Reality can bite me. There will be ample opportunity to take the high road, but this could be my last chance to enjoy the *Ay ¡Caramba!, Papi* Scenic Byway. So I submit to the brash *chico* and his south-o-the-border *machismo*, to his sensual objectification and my own throbbing desire. This evening *el muchacho* and I will stroll along *Camino Romantico* and share dinner on a candlelit patio. The air will smell of tropical flowers and vanilla.

Reality can only hope there's something good on TV.

ABOUT THE AUTHOR

Jackson Lassiter grew up nearly feral in the hills of rural Wyoming, sixth out of a brood of seven sons. He believes that this early exposure to the vagaries of Mother Nature and human nature molded his sensibilities. As an adult, he has lived in Utah, Colorado, North Carolina, Washington State, and California, but has thought of the the District of Columbia as home for nearly ten years. His work, most of it touching on the theme of living as an outsider, has appeared in numerous literary journals and anthologies, including *South Loop Review; Harrington Gay Men's Literary Quarterly; Heartland Review; Best Gay Love Stories; Apocalypse Literary Arts Magazine; Gay City; Silver Boomers; Cutbank Review; Sin Fronteras; Empty Shoes; Yalobusha Review, Spirits; Poppyseed Kolaché; DuPage Valley Review; Prime Mincer; Shenandoah Review* and *Gertrude 17.* He is the recipient of the 2009 Larry Neal Fiction Award sponsored by the DC Commission on the Arts and Humanities, PEN/Faulkner Foundation, and National Endowment for the Arts. He has won several fiction contests including *Binnacle* and *Shenandoah Review* and has been privileged enough to be invited to participate in several juried workshops.

ACKNOWLEDGEMENTS

Thanks are due to:

Jennifer, whose fingerprints are nearly as conspicuous as mine on most of these pages; to Yuri for keeping me sane (not an easy job, but someone's gotta' do it); to Ed, Carl, Kristin, Jonah and Fred, Scott, Tony Dortch, Mark and Stevan, and countless others for your encouragement and consistent support; to the amazing writers who have helped me through the years, particularly my brilliant peers in The George Washington University Department of English, Jenny McKeon Moore Community Writing Workshops; to the editors who have worked with me to make my words better; to my mother who encouraged me at any early age to read and write; to my sixth grade homeroom teacher, Mrs. O'Neill, for her gentle encouragement; to my dog, Missy, and my cat, Elliott, for being there when I needed to be distracted and forgiving me when I was so focused I ignored them.

Made in the USA
Charleston, SC
11 May 2012